First Edition Paperback

ISBN 978-0-6456898-7-7

DAYDREAMINGS:

A COLLECTION OF CONNECTIONS

First Edition Paperback

NEPTUNE HENRIKSEN

Edited by

Mireille Stahl

Published by

Neptune Henriksen

Key

0 = Coarse language

1 = Depictions(s) and/or mention(s) of death

2 = Mention(s) of self-harm and/or self-loathing (no graphic depiction)

3 = Mention(s) of emotional and/or verbal abuse (no graphic depiction)

4 = Mention(s) and/or implication(s) of sexual and/or BDSM scene(s)

4* = Depiction(s) of high impact sexual scene(s)

4** = Depiction(s) of high impact BDSM scene(s)

5 = Mention(s) of past homophobia and/or queerphobia

6 = Depiction(s) and/or mention(s) of romantic scene(s)

6* = Depiction(s) and/or mention(s) of lost and/or strained romantic connection(s)

7 = Depiction(s) and/or mention(s) of lost and/or strained platonic and/or familial connection(s)

8 = Depiction(s) of scenes that may be distressing for those with claustrophobia

9 = Depiction(s) of horror, and/or gore, and/or grotesque imagery

10 = Depiction(s) and/or mention(s) of alcohol and/or alcohol abuse

Contents And Content Notes

Additional Content Notes

These works **do not contain any** of the following:

- Slurs
- Ableism
- Misogyny
- Racism
- Transphobia
- Cissexism
- Depictions and/or mentions of **any** of the following:
    - Romantic and/or sexual relationships between adults and minors
    - Romantic and/or sexual relationships between relatives
    - Rape, sexual violence, and/or physical abuse
    - Physical violence and/or physical fighting
    - Eating disorders and/or body-shaming
    - Anything relating to emetophobia

Foreword

This collection explores intimacy in its many forms. It shows friends, family, lovers, and others. It shows moments of joy, times of darkness, the connections we make and miss.

I hope that some or many of the works in this collection resonate with you, sit with you, help you to feel seen, understood, and hopefully, less alone.

As someone who's often struggled to connect with others, I usually end up the observer, the one lost in my head watching the landscape go by on the train.

And so, to be able to take some of the scenes that I find myself lost in, over many observations, to give them little legs and see how they stand, and to think that seeing them however briefly, might stir something in you, well that's something very special to me.

A hope I always had, in many ways.

Thank you very sincerely for supporting me and my work with the purchase of this collection.

And, if I do succeed in helping you feel less alone, know there's so many out there like me, like you, like and unlike us both, and the world is big and beautiful.

You deserve to be seen by as many people as you possibly can.

The mortifying ordeal of being known is worth it, I promise.

Additional Note: December 2022

It's interesting reading these works now. There's something fascinating about how they speak to so much of the trauma of the Covid Pandemic, despite being written just before. And yet, some of these works have a feeling that they were written from such a different time.

Personally, I've grown so much since writing these pieces, that reading some of them feels like showing someone my teenage diaries, while other pieces feel like I could've written them yesterday.

Regardless of the time, trauma, and growth experienced since writing, I remain incredibly proud of this collection, and stand by it as my debut work of prose.

My above sentiment also remains, and I'll reiterate: The mortifying ordeal of being known is **truly** worth it, I promise.

Keyhole

In my dreams we fuck to Nirvana. In a hazy daze that engulfs the day and embraces us into its void.

There's rain lightly tapping on the window, and clouds glacially circling our skies. We push and pull and grab in a moment that never begins or ends. We lose track of concepts like time, hunger, loss, pain, and the ever-encroaching grief that peppers our humanly existence.

In my dreams I hold you.

I hold you close and tightly and I don't let go. Not for flames or ice, not for chartreuse or indigo, not for everything or nothing. I wind my arms around your form, and you sigh into my grip. We stand on the end of the Earth together and laugh at death. She will try and come for us, and we shall reply: 'try your best'.

In my dreams we speak.

We converse, and chat, and muse, about every human emotion, and every eventuality, in every possible occurrence, in every feasible circumstance, that any given player in the game of life may, or may not, run into. I watch your eyes, your mouth, your mind working away on your replies, and taking in my theories, engaged as you always are, amused and eager, with a child-like wonder.

In my dreams, everything smells of sage.

The earthy, honest scent, circles its way into my senses, and lodges in my brain. Everything is so new, it's so cleansed, it's fresh and void of anything that could bring either of us harm. We slow dance accompanied by the twisting of cleansing smoke, as it travels circles around us, protecting this sacred connection for all the time it could last.

In my dreams, you are there.

You're so incredibly real and vivid that when I reach out to touch you, I feel that spark as my skin meets yours. I am given another delicious, beautiful, and agonising taste of the warmth and comfort of your embrace. I taste the nuance of your lips, as we speak, without words, of the sweetest torture.

Your presence feels so genuine, so immediate, so close in my dreams.

It's as if there was never anything keeping us apart. It's as though it all followed a different path. It's almost like I'm happy, no, more than happy. Ecstatic. A rush of ecstasy that takes far too long to escape my system. So instead, it runs rampant, leaving trace amounts in spots I never think to look. Tiny, almost insignificant pieces of all that is you. Or the memories of you.

But it's only my dreams.

And so, I wake.

I wake and I realise it was only my dreams. It was only a wish fulfilled in my safest slumber, where no one else can see. A place where no others on this planet will know of the piercing agony that exists in the bitter reminder that a dream is only a dream. That my reality is quite brutally different.

There is clouds outside, but they don't beautifully circle the skies, they merely exist, and are of no glory to me.

There are others I may weave my arms around, but none feel quite as you did, and they don't bring me any of what you brought, so I let go without any regret.

There are purifying scents, and I burn them, hoping for something akin to those slumbered visions, though the affect is of little consequence, and I become indigent.

I feel nothing and everything at the reminder that you aren't here. That you aren't real to me now, and may never be again. That whatever was is gone, and whatever attempts to be a replacement will pale in comparison.

And so, defeated, I return to my bed, in hopes of those dreams, and what they hold.

Vigorous

We moved together. Synchronised. Hot and heavy.

I grabbed onto the rib cage in front of me, firm and commanding. A gasp from its owner, and another as I pulled their short hair. Hard and dominant, tilting their head into the crook of my neck as a whimper escapes their lips.

This tilt allowing me to kiss and tease at their neck. Alternating between soft, delicate kisses, and not-so-delicate sucks and bites.

I hoped I'd leave bruises, just like last week. There's something so tantalising about seeing the leavings of our sex on their body after the fact.

"P-please..." they begged, their bound wrists straining, their untouched dick hard and wanting.

"You. Know. The. Rules." I shot back, emphasising each word with a thrust of my strap.

Abel's enjoyment crystal clear in the delicious sound they let out.

I laughed.

"Keep begging..." I continued. "Tell. Me. How. Much. You.-" I grabbed their chest for effect, and halted my thrusts for a moment. "Want it, you pathetic fucktoy."

My growls, grabs, and pause were met with such enticing squirming, panting, and whimpers, it was difficult not to go right back to hitting that good spot.

"Argh!" they protested, attempting to thrust back against me. "P-Please.. O-Osh-O-"

I moved my hand from their chest to their throat, and squeezed lightly.

"Say my fucking name." I demanded.

"Please, Oshun!" They cried out, arching back against me.

"I want to watch you." I replied.

A whimper of excitement was cut short by me sliding out slowly, and was replaced by a moan of objection.

All at once, I moved from behind Abel, turned their body, and was towering over them. Their hazel eyes wide, yearning, my face surely filled with what I'm told is a dominant smirk.

I take their body in, so pleading and beautiful. I stroke their gorgeous face; their pale skin and Nordic features being framed by their dishevelled brown hair.

I run my hand over their neck and down their body, taking in their flushed form, as their chest rises and falls with desire.

It's easy to forget that they're larger than me, physically. The way Abel folds their body, makes themselves small in my presence, the way they live to be dominated. I don't often keep in mind that they're taller and broader than me. Slightly.

I also forget how gorgeous my brown hand looks on their light skin. The contrast of it all, the way the afternoon sun hit us both so differently, the way they looked from my hands, to my face, and back, like I controlled the moon and tides. Delectable.

My brown hand moved down their chest, caressing their fleshy middle, enjoying the softness, remembering all the times I'd grabbed wildly at that abdomen.

Careful to barely graze their devil-red dick, I swiftly slotted my hand in behind their knee, and pushed it up to their chest roughly.

The look and noise I was met with, let me know that roughness was very much appreciated. And, that look and noise were appreciated by my pulsing clit, as the vibrator in my strap harness reminded me how close I was myself.

I lined that strap up against Abel, and they looked up to their tied wrists and strained against them in response, their face so flushed, they looked about ready to explode. And if I have anything to do with it, they will.

Pushing in slowly, they keened and looked back to me, rocking their hips up as best they could, trying to take in the strap faster.

In response, I grabbed at their hip with my free hand, and lay my full weight into it.

I darted my eyes back to theirs, and they seemed frozen in the moment.

"Red?" I asked, worried I'd gone too far.

"No, green, green, definitely green!"

Their expression changed to that of absolute delight, and the thought I'm still able to surprise them, caused another twitch of my clit.

"Good, then..." I pushed in to the hilt. "Don't. Fucking. Act. Like. A Little. Brat." I responded, marking my words with thrusts again, and feeling my own orgasm getting closer and closer.

I moved my hand from their hip, noting the redness underneath, taking such pleasure in that redness, and instead curled my arm under Adel's shoulder.

And there we were, locked in the embrace, face to face, almost. The height difference makes that difficult.

But I could finally lay a forceful and impassioned kiss on Abel as I thrust into them, both actions eliciting sounds that spurred me on, and filled me such a sense of beauty and power.

It took me a moment to realise the closeness meant I was causing some friction between my body and Abel's hard dick, enough to feel the pre-cum against my stomach.

"You. Know. The. Rules." I asserted, boring into Abel's eyes as though I could see through them.

I felt how that edged them closer, just as I felt it edge me closer too.

"I-I do, I kn-know the r-rules!" Abel cried out in between heavy breaths. "I won't, I-I w-won't. I-I w-wanna be g-good for y-you!"

And that was it.

Watching them struggle to hold back their orgasm, and saying how they wanted to be good for me, sent me over the edge, and the hot, satisfying, pleasure-filled spasms ran through my pussy, pushing along my thrusting, as they often did.

"Ah, fuck!" I called out, collapsing my head against Abel's shoulder, as I tightened my grip all around them. "I'm. Cumming."

Within a thrust or two, I felt Abel's orgasm spill out between us, their legs gripping me between them, closing what little gap we had between us.

My orgasm continued to surge through me, pushed along by my thrusting and feeling Abel's enjoyment.

Our shouts and moans filled the small room of my flat, and I was damn happy I'd put on some music to drown us out somewhat.

As I felt the pleasurable spasms fade, and I slowed my thrusting, I looked up to Abel. Their face still rosy, as they come back down to Earth.

I move up slightly and they meet me in the middle for a soft, slow, kiss.

Crowded

I'd debated not getting on the train. I could get the next one, but I didn't want to be late, not again. Sharon already must think I'm a flaky mess. Not that she was alone in that assessment.

So, I'd got on. I'd shuffled on like the rest of the penguins, all having somewhere so important to go.

Packed in so tight, I can feel the nameless person next to me breathe, all because Transport For London doesn't think the 8:45am Overground from Hackney Central was necessary on this cloudy Friday.

If TFL had seen the platform, they'd know differently.

And I stand, tucked in closely with the other strangers, all trying to get to our destinations, and adhere to our plans.

There's someone behind me, almost touching my hand with theirs as we hold into the railing. Someone in front of me, I'm almost pressing my breasts up against their back. Someone to the side of me, almost touching my butt as their hand hangs by their side.

All so very cosy, but not actually engaged. Not actually touching, caressing, holding, not the way my body screamed out for.

No one acknowledges how bizarre this is. Being so cramped in with strangers for the six minutes it takes to get to Highbury & Islington. Staring at the back of someone's head, looking down to someone else's shoes, realising someone's managed to fit their dog on this train somehow.

And we all stand here, tightly, closely, intimately. Yet, I'll never see these people again.

This is London.

Even if I had the exact same commute every day, there's no way I'd see the same people.

It doesn't work like that here.

There are too many people, too many stories, too many variables, all lending themselves to the fact that I stand here, on this train, for a few moments, so incredibly close to these people I'll never see again.

Closer than I sit with my friends, as we lay around each other's share-house rooms, playing cards and snacking on whatever we've whipped up that day.

I love those three more than I love peanut butter, and I've eaten peanut butter every day since I was six, I'd die without it. My body would genuinely shut down, no doubt.

But those three, when we connect, we don't stand so close I can feel the heat of their bodies. They're not very touchy-feely types.

It must be that British disposition.

And as much I got out of our friendships, it felt lonely.

I was just another face commuting somewhere, for some reason, another nameless no one in a sea of other nameless no ones. That's all I felt most days.

Without a special someone, or a few special someones, it seemed there was no one to touch me.

To sit my legs on while we watched TV, to hold my hand while I cry, to sit up close to me so our thighs touch.

It wasn't about sex. It was about a sure sign that we were connecting.

I need that physical confirmation. And I'm not one to push others.

If they're not huggers, no hugs for me.

If they're not hand-holders, no holding hands for me.

If they don't like lying all over each other, we'll sit up next to each other.

I don't feel I'm missing out, but I do feel disconnected from those friends.

We'd talk about childhoods, and mental health, and our wildest hopes for ourselves, but it all felt so sterile without that physical contact.

Maybe I was just making up for lost time, or carving out a reality I was denied as a child, but it's who I am. And despite my understanding and respect for who my friends are, something was always missing.

I hear the third ding, and I'm shaken from my wondering thoughts.

This is my stop.

And so, with the herd, I shuffle off, they shuffle off, and we all go about our days.

Afternoon

I rolled onto my front, and enjoyed the feel of Rajesh's still fresh bedsheets on my face. Try as we might, we didn't manage to fully sully them last night.

Letting out a sigh, I felt a stirring behind me.

Humming to himself, Rajesh dances light touches across my shoulders, and I close my eyes to experience the sensation more fully.

Soothing, loving, a little ticklish.

I began to hum with Rajesh, smiling to myself. He responds by placing light kisses from my neck, to my shoulders, to the small of my back.

Such a content connection, such an ease of nakedness and closeness.

I turn onto my back, with Rajesh making space for me, as he always does. He strokes the outside of my thigh with the back of his hand, while gracing my tummy with chaste kisses.

Humming together, I revel in the intimacy of his gentle kisses. Not just the physicality of it, but what it reaffirmed to me about Rajesh's tactile and kind nature. His beauty, his strength, his passion for me.

Looking down at him, I realise Rajesh has folded himself up, and was propping himself up on one arm awkwardly, so as to not to place his weight on me, no doubt.

Though I did appreciate his awareness of his body, and the way he was always so tentative and controlled, I did wonder how much he was often sacrificing his own comfort for mine. Or maybe he was just enjoying whatever we were doing so much, that his dead arm, or cramped foot, or hanging leg, didn't even register.

I reach down to run my hand through Rajesh's thick, dark, hair, as his humming fades, in favour of a low and soft sigh. I run the back of my hand up and down the side of his cheek, as he closes his eyes and lays his head on my side for a moment.

These lazy Saturdays. There was nothing like it. Having the time to just lay and touch and kiss each other. To be present and share my body with someone. Someone like Rajesh.

He soothed me. Calmed me. Centred me. Made me feel like there was nothing else but the two of us.

Is it love? Lust? Perhaps more, Perhaps less.

There was always a sense that we just fit. We got each other. We spoke the same language. We were two people who felt completely at home together.

What else is there?

I gesture for Rajesh to move up, and he knows I'd like to feel his body on mine. He holds himself over me for a moment, and I reach up, pull his face to mine, and share we a short, loving kiss.

He lowers himself down, nestling his head in between my breasts, wrapping his arms up to hold my shoulders, and one leg resting on mine. Just the way I like it. He knows me so well.

Catching my eye quickly, he knows he's done well, and settles in.

I smile down at Rajesh, and bring one hand over to run fingers through that glorious hair, and place the other on his shoulder, with my thumb lazily moving back and forth.

I love the way his body looked on mine. His light brown skin resting on my deep, dark tones, and us both resting on the crisp white sheets of his bed. Our beautiful brown bodies, highlighted by the sheets, laying on clouds together.

Two angels floating through the sky.

And we stayed there. Me, running a hand through Rajesh's hair, and feeling his body wrapped around me. And Rajesh, smiling against my skin, giving me occasional calf rubs with his foot.

Connection. Intimacy. Love?

Something very important either way.

The rejuvenating power that this person has, it's so very remarkable. He refills my tank, listens to me talking about some idiot on the train, jokes along with me about some ridiculous advert.

Oh yes, this person wants to just connect with me, to lay here in bed with me.

Skin on skin, soothing touches, two bodies. So simple yet so meaningful.

"Hey." I said to Rajesh.

He looks up.

"Hey yourself."

Haze

When I look back, I can remember hearing the news.

Then, flashes of faces, interiors of shops, the work ute my mother used to drive.

There's the moment I tried to go back to school, holding my uniform and crying into the scratchy fabric.

There are the movies we watched to try and pretend it wasn't happening, some so clear, but for others, I can't remember a single scene.

There's standing up at her funeral and speaking, surprised by how unsteady my voice was, my friend squeezing my hand.

So much I can recall, and so much that's gone. Lost in the blur of the events, floating off in the wind of that deep, dragging, sadness, that sat in my stomach and still refuses to budge.

And here we stand, years and years past, our lives supposedly moved on, but our souls forever connected by this gravestone, and this small country town.

I reach out and hold Rochelle's hand, like she held mine at the funeral, or when I was in the hospital for my appendectomy, or when we would sing along to Fall Out Boy during car rides, or the thousands of other times we told each other we're still here.

She squeezes in response, and I try to wipe away my tears, sniffling and spluttering in a way that would feel uncomfortable around anyone else.

A tissue appears in front of me, and a smile from Rochelle shows me that my best friend feels it too.

Two teens hit by the same loss, filled with guilt over their sadness, because we'd only lost a friend, after all. Other people had lost a cousin, or a sibling, or a child.

And what did we lose that day? Just some friend.

So maybe we're not allowed to be sad.

Maybe this isn't our hurt to claim.

And we both carried that as we grew up. As we moved to new cities and met new people who didn't know what happened in our high school. They didn't know we had one of **those** stories.

The stories that stop the party, that kill the mood, that make the other people feel obliged to say something nice, and to tread lightly around us, like we'll shatter into a million pieces any second.

And hey, maybe we will.

Would that really be so bad?

Are people really so scared of emotion that the fact my friend fucking killed herself should remain some shameful secret?

They're just tears, they won't hurt anyone.

"We're growing up." I state, squeezing Rochelle's hand in return.

She looks at me and smiles through her own tears.

"We're old as fuck." She laughs, wiping one of her tears with a tissue.

"Got proper jobs and shit." I laugh back.

"Real grown-ups." She retorts, her tone becoming more serious and wistful.

"You're doing amazing at work, shacked up with your boy." I say, leaning over to nudge Rochelle with my shoulder.

"And you're living it up in London." She replies, nudging me back.

"Almost." I clarify.

"Come on, you're fucking crushing it!" Rochelle encourages. "You're out there chasing your dreams. How many people are doing that? You're already winning just from that."

I smile as the words hit me, and I realise something.

"I thought it would be Bianca. She was far more talented than me." I state, gesturing towards the gravestone in front of us, welling up once again.

Rochelle doesn't say anything, she just pulls me into a hug, and we stand there together.

Adults and teens.

Grown up but not grown apart.

Friends then and now.

I'm back at the funeral all those years ago. The sun beaming down on a hot February afternoon. The sky blue and clear, the grass only green in the cemetery, but golden and dead elsewhere.

Classmates and teachers filling the scene. School uniforms and dark formal attire making my red dress stick out more than intended.

A slight breeze, a welcome respite from the relentless ball of fire above, and bringing with it the scents of all the fresh flowers lain out in this new part of the graveyard.

Voices and colours and smells so vivid, yet so distant.

Rochelle gives a final squeeze, and begins to pull us apart, and I'm back in our overcast day this February, the cemetery empty except for us. A highlight reel of our road trip from Adelaide, playing in a split second in my mind's eye.

I look down at the gravestone, see the dates, think of how much has changed since then.

"Fifteen years." I simply say.

Rochelle breathes a heavy sigh.

"Yeah." She replies.

"We used to rent movies from a fucking shop." I reminisce.

"And it was such a big deal." Rochelle replies.

"Go to the Video Ezy, grab the movies." I start.

"Go to the Coles, grab the snacks." She adds.

"Go to Bianca's house, have the movie night!" We say together.

Tableaux of Bianca dancing around her kitchen in pyjamas, grabbing popcorn from the microwave, pouring and spilling soft drink on the kitchen bench, all swam into my mind for a second. Almost as if those nights of carefree teenage shenanigans never stopped.

Instead, we had less and less of them. We'd claim we were getting so busy with school work, we didn't have weekends free for movie nights like we used to.

But mostly, it was an inability to be carefree, to feel like teenagers. We'd lost so much, we'd aged years in an instant, and had no desire to regress to such shenanigans. Especially the type that reminded us of who we'd lost.

"Natalie?" Rochelle snapped me out of my musings. "I've gotta get more tissues from the car." She sniffled.

"Oh yeah." I replied, handing her the keys.

I watch Rochelle trudge to the car, through the wet, vibrantly green lawn, under a grey sky, before turning back to the gravestone.

The worry of sitting on the cold, damp ground, and how uncomfortable I could be in a few minutes time, seems completely insignificant as I settle into the clammy grass and press my hand to the dewy stone, running my fingers over the immortalised image of my teenage friend passed.

The other visits flash in my mind, so consistent at one point, now so uncommon. And moving to the other side of the world didn't help their frequency.

A sting of all-too-familiar guilt runs through me, and I silently apologise for my absence.

Fresh tears run down my cheeks as I stare at the photo, and a soft tap causes me to look at my shoulder.

Another tissue appears, and I look up to Rochelle, as she bobs down next to me.

"I know." She says.

Car Ride

"Anything happening on Facebook, Aaron?" I ask, seeing him close the app at my words.

"Yeah." He replies, distant and moody as ever. "Nuclear war, memes, trans stuff, you know."

Do I know?

"Ah, right." I keep my eyes on the road.

"Are you gonna marry my dad or what?"

Whoa. I thought we'd ease into that, but I guess not.

"Well, Aaron, it's ah... I mean, I'm sure it's an adjustment for you-"

"I don't care that you're gay, or my dad's gay, or you're both bi, or whatever, man." Aaron interrupts. "I wanna make sure that you're gonna stick around, you know?"

This wasn't what I was expecting.

Was he serious? Was this just teenage angst? Was I supposed to be able to tell the difference?

"Ah... right, ok... Well..."

"It's like, why are we even going to IKEA, anyway?" Aaron jumps in.

"So... well... I thought it might be nice for us to get Nathan- I mean... y-your dad... a dining table, and have it all put together by the time he gets back. What do you think?" I offer.

"Yeah, cool."

"Cool?" I ask, not sure what that even means right now.

"Dude, I've got my answer, ok? You clearly do care about him, or you wouldn't try and do some dumb shit like this." Aaron gestures vaguely at the car, then looks out the window.

Thanks?

"Dumb.... sh... shit?" I ask, a little hurt and surprised, but trying not to show it too much.

"What would you call trying to bond with your boyfriend's son while making that boyfriend a table... all in a day?" Aaron shoots me a look, it's off-putting and I worry I'm in too deep.

"Well... I mean... maybe not d-dumb sh-sh-shit... but... I see your point."

"It's dumb 'cause it's foolhardy or whatever... and it's romantic or some shit, I get it, dude." Aaron returns to looking out the window.

"T-thanks... and you can just call me Billy."

"Isn't Billy a bit...?" Aaron looks back to me, and gestures accusingly.

A bit straight? A bit boyish? A bit... what?

"I mean you're like fifty or whatever." Aaron strikes.

"Excuse me, Aaron, I'm forty-six." I reply, trying to be stern, but not too stern.

21

"So, what's a forty-something doing calling themselves Billy, shouldn't you go by Bill by now?"

"Aaron, I think you're being a little bit rude." I firmly but calmly point out.

"Rude?" Aaron accuses.

"Yes." I remain firm.

"Of course I'm being fucking rude, Billy!"

The look I shoot Aaron isn't pretty, it's panicked and confused.

"Billy, this isn't gonna work if you let me walk all over you." Aaron clarifies.

"Y-y-you... but..."

"Come on, Billy. You're a good dude. Anyone can see that." Aaron has completely softened his face; it's horrifying and impressive. "You're making all this effort right now to do something nice for dad, who you've only known for like... a minute. But I'm not gonna let my dad be with some Yes Man."

I sit in the wake of Aaron's words for a moment. The boy had pulled my leg so much it had basically detached. What kind of mastermind is Nathan raising? Or is this completely on Aaron?

Just a kid trying to protect their parent? Understanding the delicacy of coming out, divorcing, being on his own for the first time in years?

"Don't be so impressed." Aaron cut through my thoughts. "The last guy didn't even get past this first test."

Jazz Bar

And here we are, a hypnotic, intoxicating song that is new to me, communicating an emotion I know all too well.

The sound draws me in, holds me there, courses through me as I close my eyes and fall under its spell.

I began dancing, swirling and winding my hips, caressing my lower half just so, accentuating those womanly shapes and curves, in the manner I'd always done with Reggae, but this was different.

The cool Jazz told a different story, and my movements reflected it.

A sadness, a desire, a longing, an unrequited something that I knew was brewing.

The tempo of my hips' movements is salacious, delicious, and inviting. I know all too well the way people note my movements, the way they took notice but pretended not to take notice at the same time.

I read in their faces, the feeling of being somehow so very enticed, while so very hesitant. Frozen. Watching.

And all the while I pretend not to see. As I feel the power, the unrelenting hold I have on any and all on-lookers, as they watch my form glide through the sound, and translate the drums, horns, and piano into something they can't keep their eyes off.

I give a sly glance to Sean, aware of his eyes on me, I take a beat to realise I shouldn't lay it on too thick. So, I change my movements to something sillier, based in shimmy and steps, not purely a signal of my sexual prowess.

A playful expression is communicated, and he smiles. Bashful, sure, but not so much that an invitation for him to join me would be seen as untoward.

And like clockwork he stands, feigning resignation as he delightedly bounces over, and we begin to explore the music together.

I offer my hand in a camp and playful way, and he accepts with similar silliness. We begin by spinning each other in and out, keeping notable distance in an attempt to pretend this is what friends do.

Clearly, Sean has no idea what he's doing, so I take the lead, taking us through a simple box step, in half time, to match the soothing tones of the Jazz in this romantically lit, dream-like room.

I'm obviously showing off some flare with a hip flick here and a body roll there, but Sean's surprisingly flare-filled himself. This white man has a few moves.

Watching him for a moment, I realise my gaze has settled on his belt buckle, which is only because that's where the movement is coming from.

And anyway, Sean's so much taller than me, I have to make a real effort to look him in the eye, so what am I going to do? Stare at his shoulder? Talk to his nipples? Imagine what I might do to those nipples? What kind of pleasure or pain he might like inflicted on those nipples?

Am I supposed to not think about grabbing his body and wrestling him down, holding his hands above his head, while I kiss him passionately, grinding my hips against his, on that hotel room bed, that isn't very far from this Jazz bar?

Sean's not thinking about that, he's dancing with a friend.

Sure, Daphne Johnson is an interesting, layered, sexually-invigorated, artistically-engaged, and well-fucking-spoken, emotionally intelligent friend, who's dancing with him to these soothing and time-stretching sounds, but she's a friend.

I'm a friend.

Nothing. Can. Happen.

Nothing.

We can't do that to Anne, not to David and Isabelle. Not to my opportunities and Sean's career. Not to the fucking concept of 'can men and women really be just friends?'.

Not to the piece of shit insinuation, that a younger woman of colour is some magical fucking vixen of the night, that's going to steal some trusting innocent white woman's man, for the fucking thrill of it.

No.

I'm a friend. And we can dance. So, we will.

There's space for a whole other person in between us. Sean's hand is on my shoulder, and mine on his. We're not even touching waists. We're barely making eye contact.

And! We're making silly faces. As we giggle.

Like friends do. Because. That's. What. We. Are.

We can dance. We're allowed to dance.

And to... slow the pace of the box steps into a more natural swaying. To find each other's eye line for a moment in the dimly lit, warm, inviting, Jazz joint, as we feel the music out together, and we step a little closer with each sway.

It's just logical, that my arm would slowly gravitate to Sean's waist, where it rests, for me to better guide his fluid swaying.

That's just me syncing his movements with mine, explaining with touch, finding the bridge between each other and creating a mutual understanding. It's nothing more.

Closer and closer we move to each other, so gradual it's almost unnoticed, isn't it? I'm certainly not noticing it, and Sean's probably not noticing it, and everyone else in this atmospheric venue is too busy to notice it.

We're close enough that I can feel the heat of Sean's body, and the thought of that form under the collared shirt, and I'm sure subsequent undershirt, makes my bottom lip tingle, like friends do.

I'm sure he can feel me too, sure he can sense that tingle, and maybe he's having a similar tingle.

What's a tingle between friends?

What's a tingle between friends who are standing so painfully close that they can feel each other's warmth, the breath from each other's tingly lips, the sway and swirl of each other's hips, as they move just far enough away but so very very close?

All I can see is Sean's lips, all I can think of is a meeting of those lips to mine and the passion, power, and desire I'd show him during that meeting. How very close I'd hold him during that meeting. How I'd move my hand around to the small of his back, holding him firmly against me, pressing my body against his, raising my leg slightly to cause that little bit of friction between my thigh and his hardening cock-

Something changed. Something isn't right. Something-

The music!

It's being replaced with clapping.

I should clap. Sean should clap.

Everyone should stop whatever the fuck they're doing and clap.

Clap you fucking fools.

Clap for these wizards of sound and time.

Pounding my hands together, I realise that the crowd has thinned out and it was only a few other couples along with Sean and I.

Other couples? We're not a couples!

I'm suddenly very hot as I realise what we've potentially done.

What we've both potentially thought.

What we might have done if that final song was a minute longer.

Can I look at Sean? Should I look at Sean? Will he look at me?

I chance it and turn back towards him.

Where's Sean? He was right next to me!

"Got your jacket and bag." A familiar, steady voice, says behind me.

"Oh yeah, thanks!" I chirp in response.

I'm not sure what else to say. I guess we're going to walk back to the hotel like nothing happened?

But then again, nothing did happen. And maybe it was very much one-sided. Sean seems unaffected. He doesn't seem like he's waking from a dream, like a spell was broken, like a moment was re-contextualised in a split second.

I fold my jacket over my arm, it's too warm to need it, but I'm glad I brought it, you never know.

But looking over to Sean, I notice something.

"Where's your jacket?!" I blurt out louder than intended.

"Oh, oh yeah, it's in my backpack." He replies, turning slightly, and pointing to that very backpack.

The straps somehow mixed in with his shirt and I didn't even see it there. Or maybe I couldn't see anything else.

How can he see anything else?

Why am I the only one affected by this time-bending, enchanting, Jazz bar?

Pride & Pain

I tapped my card on the Oyster reader, and with Diem following me, we made our way through the winding channels of commuters and out into Trafalgar Square.

The sudden natural light, though dulled by the clouds, was a little much for me, and I searched for my sunglasses, only to notice Diem wasn't right behind me anymore.

"Diem?" I called out, donning my sunglasses in the busy London streets.

Turning and circling around myself, I still couldn't see her.

"Diem?!" I called again, this time more desperate and worried.

"Let's just go home, Winnie." A small voice in the crowd pleaded.

Diem was a few steps behind me, looking at her feet, shuffling them back and forth as the faceless tunnels of people passed around us.

I held out my hand, Diem took it, and I lead us to a nearby bench, which I was pleased to see had enough space for us to both sit, despite the busy scene around us.

"Why should we go home?" I asked Diem, holding her hand firmly and trying to catch her eye.

Diem told me everything she needed to by pulling her hand back, and ripping her Pansexual flag headband off, then flipping her bag to the front, and shoving the headband inside.

She sat the bag on her lap and stared blankly ahead. There was almost no trace of the brash, lively, no-holds-barred, twenty-something friend I knew so well, it was as If she'd shrunk right before my eyes, into a younger version of herself, a version I'd never met.

"Diem, come on... no, no, no." I pleaded.

"I-I... I wanna... go home." She mumbled in that same small voice.

"You belong here, Diem..." I tried to reassure.

"I... wanna... go home." She insisted, her voice getting smaller and smaller.

"It's your Pride too, Diem." I kept trying, reaching my hand out a little to a stony Diem. "Please, please... please."

I felt the tears welling in my eyes, and could see them in Diem's, despite keeping her gaze ahead, and her arms folded over her backpack.

My reached hand hung between us, as she continued to avoid eye contact and shut me out. I let my hand drift down, and it sat in the small space separating us in the crowded scene of Central London.

"Let's just go home, Winnie." Diem requested, her voice shaking. "I don't belong here, and we both know it."

"No... no, no, no." I implored. "Please don't say that. No one is going to challenge you, and if they do, they're the bad one, not you."

"I'm lying to myself." Diem mumbled as she turned to me.

"What?" I asked, shocked by the sudden turn as much as the words.

"That's what my mum always said: I'm lying to myself." Diem reiterated, her voice cold and almost calm.

The tears fell from my eyes as Diem's quote sank in.

"She's wrong, Diem, she's speaking from a place of fear and a place of-" I wiped my tears away. "-a place of ignorance. She's not speaking from a place of love."

"Why can't you just like boys?" Diem continued to quote, almost robotic in her words. "Only boys, that'll be so much easier for you anyway! And I've never even seen you with a girl, so what's all this?"

I shook my head at the quotes, at the speech Diem has clearly beat herself up with for so very long. I saw the scared teenager in there, I saw the pain and self-hatred she'd felt and internalised, when all she was trying to do, was be honest with her own mother.

A rage, powered by a thousand slurs, marked by hundreds of looks and mutters, outlined by internet comments and overhead conversations, bubbled and boiled inside me.

I wanted to shake this mother. I wanted to slap her and watch her dramatically fly across the room, like in a soap opera. I wanted to call her every horrid thing on the planet. I wanted nothing more than to make her beat herself up like she so awfully did to her daughter. I wanted her to feel such intense inner pain that she too had scars on her arms and tried to deny who she was for a decade.

But she wasn't here now, Diem was. My best friend. My soulmate in this life, and the next. My family. My heart. My everything.

"Anything and everything she ever said to you is real, and has happened." I began, looking as far into Diem's soul as I could. "But all of it, every last word, is one perspective, from one person. And you, you are your own person, you don't have to believe a word anyone else tells you."

I continued to look into Diem's eyes, not sure if what I said was even reassuring, let alone helpful, or positive.

Then all at once, we were in an embrace, holding desperately onto each other. Speaking all the pain we already knew, flashing back to the darkest and brightest moments, remembering everything we've been through and how strong our friendship remains.

"I love you too much to take you home, this is your Pride." My muffled words barely made it to Diem's ears, but she tightened her grip as recognition.

"This is my Pride." She muffled back.

I pulled us apart.

"This is your Pride."

She wiped her tears away, but held onto one of my hands.

"This is my Pride."

I bent down to catch her eye.

"This is your Pride!"

She nodded.

"This is my Pride!"

"Louder!"

"THIS IS MY PRIDE!"

"Whose Pride is it?"

"MINE!"

"WHO'S?!"

"MINE!"

We shouted and laughed, then embraced again.

I pulled back and looked at my best friend.

"Will you do me a favour?" I asked.

Diem nodded.

"Please wear your headband."

Diem smiled.

I wished she didn't have to push through so much to stand in Trafalgar Square and tie a Pansexual flag headband around her head, but I was so happy to see her do it.

"Hey, Diem?" I called.

"Mmm?" She replied, fixing the headband.

"I'm really proud of you."

Waking Up

Sometimes I think about waking up with you. I think about the soft, winter's morning light caressing your face, as it tries it's best to get around the blinds and into the bedroom.

You look over to me, and smile with a sweetness in your eyes that never loses its potency, no matter how often you show me such love.

I reach a lazy hand to gently caress the side of your cheek, and you close your eyes for a moment, taking in my touch. I smile back, but your closed eyes don't see me. I suspect you know, all the same.

I make my way to the kitchen, and begin whipping up breakfast for you and your kids, while you wake them up and get them dressed.

The soft chatter of momentary protests from them, and your patient soothing, drifts into the kitchen; while I press down the coffee, and the smell of hash browns, vegan sausages, and baked veggies, swims around the room.

You walk the two younger kids into the kitchen, and your teenager follows, scrolling through a phone and greeting me with a grunt.

We all chatter about dreams we had, plans for today, and your eldest shows me a funny tweet, while we all dig in, and you cut up your youngest's plate.

There's a sense of chaos that would've bothered me a few years ago, but with you there, and everything that you are, it feels so different.

I feel a sense of peace, I'm feeling balanced and capable, I'm... dare I say... content?

You wash the dishes, while I get dressed, and your kids brush their teeth and grab their lunches.

Among the well-oiled machine that is our morning routine, there's a moment to sneak in a hug. And so, I hold you from behind, while you stand over the sink, and I feel you dip your current dish back into the water, and lean back slightly against me.

I kiss you on your shoulder, before going to check your kids are ready, and help your youngest get their shoes on.

Looking up, you're ready to walk them to the bus stop, so I give you a swift kiss on the cheek, and see you all out the door.

With a soft click, a silence falls within the house, and I remember when that was all I ever wanted.

How I'd long for the silence, walk faster and faster until I was at the door of my flat back in London. How I'd sometimes struggle with the key, and I could feel my heart race with such of force that it felt as though I'd never be able to exhale.

Then, I'd hear the first click, letting me know the door was unlocked, and between that and the second click of it closing behind me, it was as though time stretched into a hundred embarrassing incidents, a thousand gawking stares, a million missteps and misspoken moments.

And finally, that last click.

It told me I was safe.

I was alone.

No one was looking, no one was listening, no one was judging. I could simply **be**.

Now, that silence feels the same as helping your youngest with their shoes, as laughing at the tweet your teen showed me, as hearing about to the dream your middle child had.

It's all ok, I'm ok, and it's because of you.

It's why your sweet smile warms my soul, why your patience is so beautiful, why holding you feels like home.

My thoughts are broken by the sound of your phone, where I see a text from Alex, about bringing your kids over a day early this week.

I go into the kitchen, to check our schedule for the week, and see that'll be no problem. And I replying saying as much, and letting Alex know it's me.

You return, and I call out from the kitchen, you come stand in the doorway, I offer you more coffee, and fill you in about the change with our schedule.

You thank me, I top up your coffee, and I sit on one of the stools at the kitchen island, placing your cup next to mine.

I look over, and see you're still in the doorway, relaxed but observant.

There's a moment of silence, both looking at each other in the clouded winter morning, and you smile as sweetly as ever, tell me how beautiful my soul is, and approach me at the island.

You take my body into your arms, and I rest my head against your chest. I run my fanned hands up your back, and you give out a soft sound of comfort. And we stay like that, for a few moments.

Mentored

"You make me feel so... calm." I tell Anders, looking up into his clear blue eyes.

I take his hand in mine and squeeze it, not sure what else to do, as the tears trailed down my face and I looked to our hands, instead of showing him my face, and have him see me fall completely to pieces.

Anders squeezes back, taking a step towards me, and closing the gap between us that screamed a thousand goodbyes.

"Sophie..." He trailed off.

He tried to start a number of sentences, not sure what to say or how to say it. Just a man trying to talk to a woman, in this vast, impersonal, freezing, airport.

I could feel him wanting to connect, like he had a number of times over the past month.

I'd been patient. But that patience has to run out at some point.

And it's not the time. He has work to do on himself. And I won't do it for him. He knows I'm too aware to take such a bullet for someone else, no matter how I feel about them.

Who would've thought that what brought us together would keep us apart?

"We make a good team." I said, interrupting Anders' stuttering, in between his pauses and fidgets, and looking up to him finally. "You know how I feel. I love who I am around you. I can't wait to have hundreds more conversations. But we need to make the line clear. I need to make the line clear."

Anders nodded vigorously. Furrowing his brow and trying to keep his teary eyes from wetting his cheeks.

I drew him into an embrace, and held us there for a moment.

Did I love him? Did he love me? Were we both just lost souls floating around the world, hoping someone else could anchor us down in the best way?

Was I just bored? Was he?

A month-long mentorship with Dr. Anders Gustavsen, and all I have to show for it is a freshly broken heart, and a friend I couldn't stop flirting with, despite that flirting never amounting to more than a hug that lasted too long.

I feel the cotton of his button up shirt against my face, I feel his arms around my shoulders, I feel his cheek atop my head.

We stay there.

Somewhere between friends and lovers, somewhere outside colleagues and family, somewhere away from the rest of the world.

I relish in holding onto this person that makes me feel so relaxed, so purposeful, who believes in my writing and my artistic point of view. Someone who I'd heard so much about as a mentor, but had no idea I'd connect with so deeply as a person.

As another sad sack with a sick brain, another human being pacing through their life, a new drug, a new therapist. Not always getting enough sleep. Often feeling like a character being written by someone else. Orbiting around our own lives. Trying to find meaning in our work.

We have our demons, and we'd bonded over them.

But bonding isn't facing those demons. It isn't opening up the scar tissue of old wounds, pulling out the shrapnel that's still lodged deep inside the flesh, piece by piece, and sewing it up again.

That's work Anders still needs to do.

Until he does, we can't even begin to talk about how this would work.

Would he open up his marriage? Would he get divorced? Would he wait until his children were grown? When are they ever grown?

Those kids are never going to stop needing him. And to have parents in the first place, something I can barely imagine.

I was so jealous. So jealous of his kids and their happy family.

Something I was never close to having.

A sense I wasn't a burden. A sense that someone was in my corner. A sense that someone truly cared about the young Sophie.

But of course, we'd talked about that. Or at least, I'd talked.

Anders had listened, and how he loved to listen.

And when I was done, he'd thanked me for being so open, said he understood where I was coming from, but that he could never truly understand my pain, and we'd sat in the moment.

It was so close, so far.

And yet, I was pulled further in.

Like I'd pulled Anders into this embrace, in this airport. With my flight leaving in two hours.

We hear something over the Tannoy. Words telling us that we can't stay like this, that this hug, just like whatever our relationship has been, has to end. We have to go back to our corners of the world. To our less-than-satisfactory existences. With our itches.

"I guess that's my cue." I state, pulling away from Anders, as he traces his arms along mine, trying to elongate the hug. "What was the gate number?" I ask, so I can wipe the tears from my face without him seeing.

"Uh... it says gate E6." He states, his voice shaking in a manner I didn't expect.

It was so hard for me to know how he felt. I could sense a pulling, a rope tethering us together, linking us somehow. But I thought maybe it was just me. It was all in my head, like so many things seem to be.

He'd never been clear, even when I asked if I should back off, because maybe flirting is inappropriate and disrespectful. I guessed he was trying to say more than just the words he'd stated, but I couldn't read between them.

And sure, he was always offering to help me carrying things, he'd rush to get the door, he'd insist on paying the bill when we'd get coffee. But he was only being polite, being a mentor, being a good host. Right?

"Well... I'd better get to gate E6." I reply, my voice surprisingly steady.

We stand there for a moment, not sure who should move first. Not sure if something else should be said. Not sure if anything will ever be said again.

"Thank you for this opportunity... Dr. Gustavsen." I state. Semi-formal, semi-playful.

"No need to thank me, I didn't do anything. It was all you... Soph- I mean, Ms. Nguyen." He responded. Equally half-formal and half-playful.

I pick up my carry-on bag, and look for the signs to gate E6.

"I was going to- I mean, if you... don't mind- I thought... I could- I mean... I could walk you?" Anders stumbled out, tilting his head slightly.

I softly smiled.

"Lead the way."

Alone in Airports

Raised voices. Thunderous footsteps. Shattering door slam.

Once again everyone was fighting. Everyone but me.

I was the youngest after all. Not that I was ever treated like it in any other scenario.

"Jade is so mature for her age!"

"Talking to her is like talking to a pint-sized grown-up!"

"Yes, she's very smart, too smart for the other kids, though."

I heard it all.

They thought I was asleep, but most of the time, I was crying silently in my room. Trying my best to avoid Their voices, Their eyes, Their opinions. Whether they were yelled or whispered, they were hurtful, alienating, reminding me that none of Them were really on my side.

I can't remember when I started to cry silently. When I learned to keep my breathing steady and my wails contained, but at some point, after the age of five and before the age of ten, it had become so second nature, I couldn't cry any other way.

And so, I would be left alone, assumed to be fine because they couldn't hear my despair.

Alone is all I ever wanted to be.

Daydreamings

Around Them, I felt watched, judged, constantly critiqued.

But alone in my room, I could pretend I was older, I was grown up, on my own in a real way.

In my mind's eye I see myself, in a small flat, in some big city.

I'd have something sweet in the oven and some music on the stereo. I'd be dancing around, enjoying my own space. Feeling free and unburdened.

Maybe even happy.

Finally, I'd have some sense of control over my life. The voices would be gone, the thudding of footsteps would be gone, the doors would stop slamming, and there'd be peace.

Peace for me. All on my own. Alone at last.

I take those thoughts, and I keep them in a special place in my brain. For the hard times. The loud times. The unhappy times.

They keep me going, they give me strength, they help me feel that one day, it will be better.

It's all I ever hope for myself, all I ever see for myself. There's no spouse, no kids, no pets. Just me.

Just me all on my own.

Decorating the place as I like, keeping it as clean as I like, making a mess when I like.

My space, my home, my refuge.

Something that's mine.

Where I can be myself. Unwatched by the judgemental eyes of Them.

I can be honest with myself about what I need in this life, about who I love in this life, about who I am in this life.

With some time and some space and some quiet. I can finally think. I can finally breathe. I can finally cry out loud.

And I'll be able to find myself, I locked her away in here somewhere.

But there, when I'm alone, I can pull her out and let her soar. She's in here, and she'll be coming out some day.

I look around my darkened room for my headphones and plug them into my phone. I haven't dared turn on the light, not even my small lamp. They might see the light under my door, and come in, giving me a piece of Their minds for being awake so late, or even worse, ask if I heard any of that fight.

I never could tell if I'd get the full brunt of their aggression or some odd forced kindness.

And I never could tell which was worse.

Do I put up with the aggression, or try and convince the kindness that I'm alright?

Either way, I never did feel I could be honest.

I never felt They could see me, any of Them.

All day at school, I'm surrounded by the other kids. All night at home, They're here. And with all those people around, it was still only me. So why want for anything but my own space?

In my own space, there's not going to be two people who ignore me, because they're too busy making their comments to each other, talking to each other through me, seeing right past me. I never needed any love, did I?

I'll find my own love, my own comfort, my own life.

Scrolling through my phone's music, I find Music For Airports, and press play. Hoping once again, that the ambient, soothing sounds, will allow my old soul and my tired brain a rest from the constant attempts to escape my reality.

With each soft note I feel my body breathe, relax, sink into my bed. I close my eyes for a moment and imagine an airport.

I'm there. I'm grown up. I'm leaving forever.

There's nothing They can do about it.

Sha-la

I plop my feet onto Drew's lap, settling into the grey couch in his lounge room.

The afternoon sun streaks in through the large window, as he takes my foot into his hands, and starts rubbing away some of the tension my body loves to hold.

We catch each other's eyes, and I begin to stroke his thigh with my other foot, as he moves his massage up and down my calf.

We smile. I wink. He makes a faux-scandalised face. I playfully kick his thigh.

We laugh.

The ukulele I'd fetched from the guest room finds a comfortable spot on my tummy, though it's trying it's best to slide around. The polyester fabric of my orange patterned romper isn't the stickiest. Who would've thought?

As I tune the uke up, and Drew continues his massaging of my feet, as he loves to do, I catch his eye.

Those deep, dark brown eyes. Peppered with flecks of orange and yellow, that show up in this sunlight. Framed as they often are, by those round glasses that I always tease give him such a 'I Love Lucy' look.

But of course, he'd love that. And so would I.

Oh, and the brown hair that I tousle at any opportunity, that soft, boyish face, that pasty white complexion. Rocking an old band tee over some cut off black jeans, like the true Skater Dad he is.

What a fucking babe. I love him with everything I have in me.

We breathe together, holding our gaze, feeling the string that pulls us together wind a little tighter. And we sit there, in the moment, with the silence around us, the day winding down, the bliss of time together doing nothing extraordinary.

Just us. Together.

Still, Drew massages my feet and calves. Speaking his love language of choice: acts of service.

He's so beautiful, I could parkour up a wall, or fight a pigeon, or just do anything and everything in my power to make him happy, like the sap I am.

I watch him for a moment, his pale hands working my warm brown skin. The contrast was always so gorgeous to me. And more obvious now, as I'm a few shades darker from all this recent sun.

"Any requests?" I ask, finishing up my tuning.

"Whatever you're feeling." He replies, smiling his trademark soft, sweet smile.

I muse for a moment, not sure what I'm feeling.

Then I have the perfect song.

"You gonna sing along?" I ask, giving him a little thigh nudge.

"Only if it's 'Für Elise' by Beethoven." He quips.

"Don't ruin the surprise!" I volley back, playfully flipping my pixie cut hair.

"Are you trying to see which one of us is more femme?" Drew teases, circling a section of his cute curls.

"No. Because you'll win, like always." I tease back.

"So true." Drew teases again, giving his best 'who me?' expression.

"You're so pretty." I state, changing the tone completely.

Drew blushes and tries to stutter out some sort of 'thank you' while trying to hide his face, despite still having one hand busy with my foot.

He makes me fall in love with him again every day.

I start strumming, moving through the chords of the intro, and Drew hasn't clocked the song until the opening line.

Then, he sees where I was going with all my teasing, and he's equal parts amused and flattered. It's clear by the way he's trying to hide his face in his shoulder.

I sing of days when the rains came, of laughing and running, and thumping hearts. Then I'm sure to lock eyes with Drew, so I can watch him melt.

"...and you, my brown-eyed girl..."

And he loves it. He loves feeling romanced. Feeling seen and wooed.

He squirms and blushes even brighter, while I smile and soak it up.

I continue to sing of transistor radios and slipping and a-sliding, and get ready for his melting once again.

"...you my... brown-eyed girl..."

Ahhh yes! More curling and wriggling, and enjoying every second of it.

As I move to the pre-chorus, I nod, encouraging Drew to sing the 'sha-la' part with me. He nods back, and I smile, biting my lip for the smallest moment.

And we 'sha-la' together. Me, so locked into those brown eyes, and the creases around them, as Drew smiles wide.

We're in it.

We're here.

We're two crazy kids in the 1960s lying in the green grass.

A part of me knew there was another verse, that the song wasn't over in someone else's mind. But this was our minds, this was my brown-eyed girl.

We moved in closer and closer, and I put the uke down somewhere as I climbed onto Drew, and held his face in my hands.

Still sha-la-ing together, I stroke his face, as he holds my calves.

I rest my forehead against his, while I sing to him, and when I lean back a little, he drops out his vocals to look up at me like he always does. Like I hold all the information in the universe. Like I could bring down every civilisation with a single word. Like I'm able to travel through time and space itself.

I slow my sha-la-ing to a halt, and hover above Drew's lips for a moment. I nudge his nose with mine, smile, then all at once I move in.

I move softly yet firm, and he follows. I taste his tongue, still sweet with the fruit salad we ate what feels like an eternity ago. I bite his lip gently, and he lets out one of his little whimpers. I turn his face, and place kisses along his cheek, feeling the light stumble. And I nuzzle his face, bringing our lips to meet for a chaste kiss.

We breathe together as our lips part.

"I mean it, you're beautiful." I state, looking him squarely in the eyes.

He tries to look away from me, always too bashful for his own good. But I hold his face and touch our foreheads once again.

"Freja!" Drew protests, trying to avoid me once again.

"Drewbert." I firmly reply.

He takes in a deep breath.

"Ok." He looks up at me, blushing beetroot red.

I chuckle.

"Beautiful."

I kiss one cheek.

"Beautiful here too."

I kiss the other.

"And here too."

And I quickly pull up Drew's shirt and lay a raspberry on his tummy.

He protests, I jump up and launch myself to the other end of the couch, poised and ready.

Drew jumps to his end, and after a moment of trading silly expressions, he playfully charges at me.

We chase each other around the living room as the afternoon sun dances around us.

Traces & Tastes

I run my fingertips along Zahra's form, the lightness of the touch making her wiggle slightly. She smiles down at me, and I kiss her hip, looking up to her.

That dark skin, rich and radiant, intoxicating and glorious.

Mainly because it was her skin. Zahra gave me so much strength, so much confidence, so much happiness, and it wasn't just me.

Anyone who was touched by her presence felt special, felt something stir in them that amplified their day, that lifted their spirit.

And I am blessed to share in her body, in all its exposed, honest, glory.

"You're so beautiful." I murmur, sleep so obvious in my voice.

She laughs, the joy filling her face, lighting up her eyes, animating her bold features. She was truly a work of art.

"I'm glad we finally agree on something." She remarks, her smile changing to a sly look of self-satisfaction.

"You're a snarky little shit, you know that?" I throw back, relishing in our playfulness and her wit.

"Well you're the girl who fell for a little shit, so who's the real winner here, Hannah?" Zahra retorts, folding her hands behind her head, like she's a white boy in an 80's movie.

"I'm the real winner, because you're an amazing human being." I state, not being able to keep the banter as fresh as she can.

Zahra looks down out of the corner of her eye, letting me know she loves that I know how lucky I am, that I appreciate her, in everything she is.

I caress my hand from the small of her back, over the folds of her waist, so prominent in her twisted position.

I feel the dips and rises in her body, like a landscape, they tell me so many stories and show me so much, yet so little.

I reach those hip stretch marks, and note their prominence on her beautiful black skin.

'...I'm midnight, deep and powerful, the witching hour'.

As she'd said on our first date.

And oh, she was.

Then, I saw that beautiful hair, defying gravity and proudly proclaiming her heritage, her identity, her essence, and I was smitten.

And oh, this was before I was even able to experience her wit, her light, her gravitas. She commands a room, and she deserves their attention.

Zahra watches me trace the lines that wrap around her hips, I caress her shapely form, and look up into her deep brown eyes, admiring her sculptural face. Her expression of amusement and admiration, with a tinge of 'this silly bitch is the best'.

I give her hip another kiss, this time slower, more sensuous, and I lock eyes with her, showing my intentions.

Another kiss, and I caress up and down her sides slowly, as she moves with me, allowing me to move closer to pleasing her.

Following with her, I kiss the insides of her thighs, teasing my lips along the sensitive skin, just how she likes me to.

Locking eyes again, I begin moving my way up her body, to some protesting moans from the queen herself. I reach her neck, and the moans change to those pleasurable sounds I love hearing from her.

Moving back slightly, I hold myself over Zahra, looking deep into her captivating eyes, and I go in for one soft kiss.

We stay there for a moment, and Zahra reaches up to stroke my back. Invoking a hum from me.

In a rushed and haphazard move, I scramble back down between her thighs, I've got to taste her right this second.

I take her clit into my mouth, slowly circling the sensitive tip with my tongue, as I've done many times before.

My movement is met with closed eyes and a head rolling back, and fuck, she looks good from down here. Her body reacting to my movement, her form moving and responding at my touch, it's wonderful.

Her delicious taste fills my senses as I continue my movement, mixing in some side-to-side, some light sucking, and some up-and-down, to ensure I don't tire myself out too early, as much as to keep it interesting.

My hands slowly dance up and down her form, gracing her thighs, her hips, her middle, caressing her chest and tracing around her nipples.

How I loved exploring her body with my hands.

In return, she moves her hips ever so slightly with me, runs her hands over mine, and reaches down to caress my face, neck, and shoulders.

It's exquisite to feel her touch as she shows me her pleasure.

Zahra's breathing changes and so does her grip on me, and I know she's getting close.

I move my hands to her hips, holding her firm, while I continue those circles that I know please her in such a delectable way.

Her breaths become subtly heavier and louder, as she holds me as firm as I her, and I manage to watch as she watches me.

Our gazes locked and powerful as she squeezes her thighs ever so slightly with each breath.

"I'm g-gonna..." she breathes.

And all at once she throws her head back, squeezes me between her thighs, digs her fingers into my shoulders, and lets out a deep, guttural groan.

I keep my movements the same, knowing changes will cut her orgasm short, and hold those hips as firm as I can manage.

Zahra looks back to me, and shows me the pleasure she's feeling. I'm filled with a mix of arousal and vicarious fulfilment as I watch her bliss paint its way across her face.

It's so satisfying to please her, watch her enjoy my mouth, my hands, my body on hers.

I used to think it'd feel like a powerful ego boost, like 'oh wow, I can make a girl cum, good for me!'. But no, it's more than that, it's another way to show how much I admire Zahra, how much I love her sense of humour, her essence as a person, her body and mind and soul.

I never feel more connected to Zahra, more beautiful in my own eyes, than when I'm causing an orgasm to pulse through her gorgeous form.

And yeah, I want to make her cum. Orgasms are fucking great.

But the slight lessening of the thigh squeezes let me know she's coming down, and so I slow to slightly longer traces, as I watch her squirm through the aftershocks, as she releases my shoulders from her grasp.

A silent conversation through touch.

I raise up slightly, and begin kissing my way up from her thighs, to her tummy, to her breasts, then to her neck, and finally, hovering over her lips.

She looks up at me for a moment, holding my face in her hands, and rubs her nose against mine. I giggle quietly, and she shuts me up by pulling me in for a powerful, loving kiss.

Zahra moans into the kiss, and I know she's enjoying tasting herself on my tongue.

Nice To Meet You

"I know we uh, we haven't... you know, always had the best relationship, kiddo." Dad piped up from the chair next to me.

We'd been sitting in silence for maybe an hour or more. And all of a sudden, he comes out with this?

"Uh, I-I guess it's been, you know, hard sometimes." I reply, putting down the crossword I was working on under these harsh florescent lights.

Dad places a hand on my shoulder. It is awkward and I want it to stop, but I can see what he was trying to do.

"You don't need to sugar-coat it, kiddo." He continues, squeezing his hand, then patting me, before stopping this stilted and strained physical touch, and pulling his hand back. "I've been... uh... what was the word... distant. I've been distant your whole life, uh, Avi."

To hear Dad use my new name was... well, new. He'd been avoiding the whole non-binary thing for months now, and since I was ok with 'kiddo', it didn't seem like something worth going to war over.

"Uh, thanks for- for calling me Avi, Dad." I manage to get out.

"Well, that's your name, ki- I mean, Avi." the old man reassures, clasping his weathered hands together and looking down at the floor. "But that's just the start, alright?"

"Alright." I reply, not sure where this new man has been all my life.

Sure, we've been sitting for hours in this fucking hospital, but how much can that have affected Dad's entire world view?

"Your mother might-" he starts up, bringing a thumb to his eye like he's trying to poke it out. "She might- might not make it, you know? And it'll just be the two of us, Avi."

Well yeah, but I assumed we'd just avoid each other every waking second, like we have for the past thirty years.

"It could be just the two of us, but, that's- that's ok, Dad." I reply, as I try to return his hand-on-the-shoulder gesture.

There's a pause in which we're both so still, and I worry he might turn to actual stone.

"Look at us, kid, we can't even talk about the only person who ties us together." He protests, looking up at me finally, and I see the tears he was trying so hard to push back in.

"It's-uh... it's-"

"It's fucking shit, Avi." he interrupts, and for once, I'm thankful for his interruption. "I've been fucking shit."

And with that, the old man slumps back in his chair and sobs softly.

His huge sheepskin coat emphasising his slowly heaving shoulders, as he bounces his booted feet like an anxious child.

It was confronting.

It was like seeing something I shouldn't.

It was **refreshing**.

A real-life human being lives inside that burly frame. Under that flannelette shirt is a genuine beating heart. Under those blue jeans are shaking limbs.

And beneath that macho man is an honest to goodness soul.

"Dad." I begin, taking his hand in mine, with a bravery I didn't have moments ago. "I don't know you, that's true. But only because I haven't really been able to see you. Until now."

The Macho Man turns toward me, his expression full of a fear I've never seen.

"I didn't mean to hide from you, kid." He admits, shame clear in his tone. "I'm- fuck, kiddo, I'm so sorry."

"I get it Dad, I get what you were told growing up, how you were raised, and how it must've-"

"You shouldn't have to, ki- Avi." He interrupts, and again, it's one of the few times it's called for. "I'm supposed to be the parent, I'm supposed to do the bloody understanding stuff routine."

He clasped his other hand over mine, and looked at me with an honesty he'd never shown me.

"I was shit." He reiterates. "I was truly shit, and I'm sorry, Avi."

A pause fills the air between us, as I wonder how to respond.

So often I've felt I need to just agree with the man, that I need to apologise for him apologising, that his word is gospel and I'm better off not speaking at all.

And then, the words come to me.

"Thanks, Dad." I say simply.

He nods.

A different man sits next to me. A man I hope to get to know. A man I'm only just meeting.

I give a weak smile, not sure what else to do, and he stands in response, holding his arms out.

I join him, and take the old man into my arms.

He's still far too rough, doing that weird back-patting thing that Dads do, but I squeeze him anyway.

We pull apart and he holds my shoulders firm, looking me over in a way he never has before. I wonder what his game is here.

"I like how, uh, boldly you dress, Avi." He gruffly grunts after a moment, gesturing to my leopard print trousers and Poet shirt, under my friend's canary yellow jacket. "I was never that brave."

"Dad, you're plenty brave." I reply, tears welling in my eyes. "And there's still time to have a little flare!"

He chuckles, it fills the stale waiting room, and I join in.

There we stand, two generations, laughing together, trying to get to know each other.

An unfamiliar voice breaks our laughter.

"Excuse me, Mr. Henderson?" A doctor called to Dad.

"Uh, yes, that's me." He stepped forward, taking his calloused hands off my shoulders. "You too!" He called, beckoning me towards the doctor.

"And you're the- uh..." The doctor began, clearly unsure how to address me.

"The child of the patient, yes." Dad answered for me, giving me a playful, and surprisingly light, nudge.

I smiled to myself, looking at the linoleum floor rather than anyone.

"Right!" The doctor proclaimed, looking back at the chart. "So, regarding Mrs. Henderson... Well, I'm so very sorry, we did everything we possibly could, but unfortunately-"

I couldn't hear anything, I could barely see anything, tears were streaming down my face, and I reached out to the sheepskin jacket, but it was gone.

He was on the floor, head in his hands, wailing into the hard linoleum.

I reached to the wall on my other side, feeling my knees buckle, and tried my best to keep myself upright.

Suddenly we were in the room with her, but she wasn't there, she was gone and the lack of machines surrounding her proved that.

Then we were in a car, making our way back to the family home, the taxi driver telling some story that fell flat on us.

At home I ordered us food, we ate in silence.

So much for getting to know each other.

Later, I lay in the guest bed, hearing the faint sounds of the crying man down the corridor, unable to sleep regardless.

Movie Night

I've never felt so alone as leaving that cinema, and hearing her exclaim her lack of interest for that film.

To have sat next to each other for two hours, having completely different experiences, it was like I'd never met her before.

The twelve years we'd been married had taken their toll, but I had pushed it aside every time.

I loved her, she loved me, and we'd worked out problems as they came up. Simple. Marriage. Done.

And in an instant, all the cracks were illuminated, so clear to me now I could kick my own arse for not seeing them sooner.

The times we'd been disconnected, that I'd brushed off as flukes, they'd all been sitting somewhere in my subconscious, waiting to be lined up one after another, all equalling something deep-seeded being wrong in our relationship.

We were supposed to be the dream team, the one and only, the power couple of everything.

But I'd been ignoring all the vignettes in which we'd stopped connecting. The kisses that missed the mark, the jokes that didn't land, the remarks that seemed in poor taste, the sex that had slowly meant less and less to both of us, the awkward pauses that replaced comfortable silences.

It all flashed in my mind's eye as I stood frozen in the cinema foyer.

I'd walked out in a daze as she'd torn the film to shreds, and I'd barely heard every few words, but felt the tone stab through me as it all fell into place.

Now, she looked at me perplexed, tilting her head to the side, moving her gaze to our surroundings, and appearing increasingly more panicked.

Her lips moved, and I'm sure she asked me something, but none of the words reached my ears. It was muffled nothingness as I stared back at her, and she moved in and out of focus, waiting for a response.

The words of critique bounced around my head, as I recalled the film's images and the way I felt so very understood as I sat in the dark next to my wife.

I moved outside of myself, and watched us watching the film, saw my looks of delight, contrasting with her faces of apprehension and boredom. The scene played in slow motion, and our faces contorted, becoming grotesque and skewed.

Our skin melted off, jolting up to the ceiling in one swift shift, as our skeletons mocked the players on the screen.

Our ceiling flesh transformed into vines which wrapped itself around everyone else in the cinema, one by one, it twisted and tangled around them, until their skulls splattered their blood and brains all over the walls, floor, and ceiling.

Their spilled flesh was consumed by our ceiling vines, joining our meat, until it was all one huge bio-morph, which made its' way to the screen and covered the attractive screen players and their gorgeous surrounds completely, so that no one could see the images flicker around the screen, and a darkness engulfed the entire room.

"Hello!" Willow snapped at me, pulling me from my visions. "Babe, can you maybe pay attention when I speak?"

"Yes, I'm sorry, I was just- I'm sorry." I reply, deciding not to explain myself. "What were you saying? I would like to hear it, and I'm sorry."

I hope my tone is genuine enough and she couldn't detect my attempts for our interaction to just be over as soon as humanly possible.

"It's ok babe, you don't have to, you know, grovel." She reassures, rubbing my arm and smiling. "I appreciate you saying sorry but, you know, I was worried you'd drifted off too far there."

"I uh, yeah, I was just thinking about the film." I replied, feeling the lack of connection even in this attempt to communicate.

"Urgh! Wasn't it the worst?!" Willow retorted, rolling her eyes.

"Yeah." I manage to reply, hoping this can be over soon, and I can go home and do absolutely anything else.

"That director is honestly super bizarre! I mean, what was up with those rabbits?" She exclaimed, punctuating her words with raised hands and contorted expressions.

"I know." I reply, hoping against hope that I can change the subject with something, anything. "Why don't we get some dinner?"

"Vivian!" Willow exclaimed, with the same level of disdain. "We ate before the movie! What are you talking about, woman?"

"Oh, yes, of... um, of course." I stammered out, wishing I could be anywhere but here. "How about some dessert then?"

"Wow, you're in a weird mood tonight." Willow replies, finally pulling back her gestures. "Zoning out, then you want two dinners, now you want dessert...."

We walk out into the warm evening, and I instinctively place my right hand on the small of her back, feeling different in a manner I didn't expect.

As we make our way down the still bustling streets of Surry Hills, I look down at the ring on my other hand, spinning it with my thumb.

Reach

From: Neptune Henriksen <████████@live.com.au>

Sent: Thursday, 18 April 2019 02:37 AM

To: ████ ████ <████████@gmail.com>

Subject: I hope you're ok

Hi,

I really want to respect your need for space at the moment, so please feel no obligation to respond to this right now or soon, though if you can let me know you've seen it, that would be really nice.

My recent responses have been super short because I was worried about putting too much on you, and making you feel a need to "get into it", whatever "it" might have been at that moment.

Because of this, I think there's been a real lack of clarity, especially when compared to our usual essay-length emails.

Usually, we've really taken the time to be sure and clear and to talk things out, when and if they were ever misunderstood.

I was assuming and hoping we would talk things out at a later stage, and now I'm not sure when later is, or if it's ever going to come along.

I'm worried that leaving things too long before we talk them out, because that creates so much more time to think about the other person's perception of what's going on, and worrying that one or both of us has hurt the other person, and I don't want to hurt you.

To be honest, I've been trying to keep this at the back of my mind, even trying to push it all the way out of my mind, thinking that not thinking about it is the healthiest thing to do. I need to allow you the space you asked for, and respect the boundary you've put in place by asking for that space.

But I keep thinking of you, and though I've adjusted to not talking to you as much as I used to, it's a difficult change to make. I didn't realise how much I relied on those emails, and how important it was to talk to someone as anxious as I am.

This may be selfish on my part, I know that, but I miss those emails so much and I hope that we can start talking it out soon.

I also know that you're finding a new therapist and changing your meds too, but I don't want you to feel like this is a time you have to push me away. This is a time you can lean on me.

You're allowed to feel overwhelmed by everything that's changing at this time, and I don't want you to feel that you have to hide any of that from me.

You say you're not a people person, but you're one of the best people I know. No one has ever made me feel so free and so supported. You make me feel I don't need to change or soften a thing about myself around you. It's not just how much you believe in me; it's also how I feel truly seen by you.

You should know, I don't keep in touch just to be nice. Not like we do. Not lengthy back and forth emails for the past year straight. It's because of how special I feel our understanding of each other is.

I'm here, and I care, and that doesn't stop just because you're making changes.

I really hope you're ok,

Neptune

Get Outlook for Android

Phone Calls

Another car ride. Another distracted mother. Another set of headphones.

Or I guess two sets of headphones, one for her, one for me. Might as well get the pair, right?

I reclined my seat and thought I should just try and get some sleep. Maybe I'd wake up in a better mood, or at least the time would go by faster. It did often seem the best way to get to the end of the day.

Behind my sunglasses, I look over to my mother, less than an arm's length between us, in this cramped hatchback. She has her hands-free plugged in, her phone between her thighs, her t-shirt on so she doesn't crease her dress shirt. An image I saw from the passenger's side since a young age.

She gestated vibrantly; her words drowned out by the latest additions to my collection of Whiny White Boy Music. Nothing like teen angst to remind you you're not alone in your teen angst.

I closed my eyes and tried to let the words wash over me, hoping to find a friend in the lyrics of some sad white boy, with whom I likely had little else in common.

A mother trying to smash the glass ceiling, trying to prove a woman of colour is just as qualified and capable as some white man. Trying to instil in me some impossible work ethic that made me worry for her health since I was old enough to speak.

70

I'd watched her get older, but still attempt to keep up those fourteen-hour days. Watched her come home, put food on the table, and try again and again to call her sleeping father in to eat with us, as he'd pester her to get remarried and have a man around the house. Like it was so easy for a half-Welsh-half-Indian, middle aged woman, with two kids, and a more than full-time job, to find a man who wasn't only seeing her as some fantasy, or some warrior.

But then again, he was a white man, he didn't get it either.

A few songs pass, and I open my eyes, able to pretend I'm still asleep under the cover of my sunnies. Looking up at the woman who somehow found the time to iron my pinafore at 1am and make a 7am meeting, I wondered if I'd ever know her.

I had heard of children who know their parents, especially as they get old enough to understand their parents were kids once, too. But that wasn't us. That wasn't my mother.

She was so busy trying to do everything herself, she didn't have time to actually talk to me.

And this was supposed to be that time. Us. Just the two of us. No boys. Girl talk.

But she was on the phone. Always on the phone. Talking to anyone but me.

She'd seemed to genuinely believe we'd get to talk this time. As she hung up her freshly pressed dress shirt in the back, and put her low-calorie snacks in her cup holder, she'd seemed so engaged in telling me about how this drive was going to be '...such a great chance for us to chat'.

Yet here I am. Sitting, or rather, laying, less than a foot away from her, and she's a thousand miles away.

But I couldn't be too hard on her, could I? I wasn't a parent; I didn't know what it was like. I was just some ungrateful little brat who does nothing but complain.

Oh yes, the regular scoldings. She'd always apologise after.

She'd say she was under a lot of pressure, say she didn't get enough sleep, say she was just hungry. There was so much traffic, you see. Someone was racist at work, but she couldn't just go saying something. Someone was sexist at work, but you've got to pick your battles. Someone drank the last of the coffee at work, but who can prove it was Simon. Someone or something else was always the cause of another one of her bad moods. And I shouldn't be so sensitive anyway.

Thanks, mum. I'm so glad we get to spend all this quality time together, being so wonderful to each other.

Being honest about the hurt you feel over your dead husband, and the loneliness you experience as a single mother.

Sharing about your unresolved childhood issues of being the only brown kid in the whole damn school, and it was a **big** school.

Opening up about the turning point when your mother had finally had enough of your father ten years ago, and had walked out on his right-wing-talking, unhelpful, misogynistic-as-they-come, armchair-critic self.

Yes, wouldn't that be so wonderful, mother? To be honest about why you're yelling at your children day in, day out.

Be honest about the fear that maybe you are unlovable, maybe you are too quick to anger, maybe you don't know the hurt you cause until it's too late.

Maybe that's why no one wants to join this household. Maybe that's why you're still having that affair with your boss's son.

Maybe that's why you need those two glasses of wine a night '...to just relax from a hard day, Gloria, what are you, my mother? Don't you know how hard I work to put food on the table, and clothes on your back? I can have a couple of glasses of wine!'

But we're not going to be honest, are we mother? We're going to keep burying things down, so deep down that they couldn't even think of surfacing any time this decade. And you'll keep me at an arm's length, while insisting we spend some quality time together.

It'll only be a few more years, and then I can move out of this stranger's house and into some share house with a bunch of dead beats who will probably drink the last of my orange juice. Out of the container. And never replace it. Or apologise.

But maybe I could at least get to know them.

Stage Empty

My hands shake as my fingers try to navigate through to call Matt.

The night was winding down around me, with only a few hangers-on stumbling around the venue's courtyard, clearly too drunk to even notice my presence, as I huddled myself on one of the picnic benches, my costumes and flyers bagged up around me.

I hold the phone to my ear, trying my best to take in a few deep breaths, and hopefully keep my voice even when he answers.

"Holly?" I hear through the phone.

"It didn't- it didn't go well tonight." I reply, willing my voice to steady.

"Uh fuck, I'm sorry to hear it." He responds, genuine compassion in his tone. "Do you want to talk, or be distracted?"

"Talk... Talk. I wanna talk about it." I blurt out, between stilted breaths.

"Yep, just a second, Other Matt and me are just watching a movie, I'll let him know- just a sec."

I hear faint voices, as he tells his same-named best friend that he might as well finish the movie without My Matt.

Other Matt says something about telling me hi, and something about needing to head off in two hours.

"Ok, I'm back." I hear, along with a click I assume is a door closing. "I'm in my room too, if that helps."

"It... it does, thanks." I reply, hearing my own voice crack through my words.

Matt has never pushed me to cry, or not to cry, he knows my relationship with it is complicated, and he just meets it with silence.

"Bad show?" He asks, his tone casual, helping me to feel safe to open up.

"Bad show." I agree, recalling the low numbers, lack of laughs, and drunken punters slumping stony-faced in their seats. "Fucking shit show."

"How many?"

"Seven. Two couples, three drunk randoms. And that's after two hours of flyering." I report.

I remember the countless faces I tried to engage about my comedy show, only to hear the same responses every time.

"I'm so fucking tired, Matt." I confess.

I take in a deep breath, I try to blink away the fresh attempt at tears, and breathe out slowly.

"It's a good show, I worked hard on it, you know that, but sometimes it feels like no one wants to see it." I admit, still getting used to such candid sharing. "I got radio interviews, rave reviews, done tons of promo spots, but I can't get people in fucking the door."

"It's fucking shit, Holly." Matt responds, caring and understanding as always. "You have every right to be tired. It sounds tiring."

"I'm putting myself out there every day, trying to get punters excited about the show, but they just don't give a shit." I reply, an anger accompanying my tired sadness. "They don't care that this is actually a banger of a show, that I put in the work for it to be a banger, they're just here to see some big name, and drink overpriced beer."

"It is a banger, I saw it go off here." He affirms, recalling the show he attended in Perth. "And Other Matt thought so too, and the friends he brought, and remember my sister loved it when she went?"

"I know, and that almost makes it worse." I respond. "Maybe if I'd started with these shitty Adelaide crowds, I would have appreciated those shows in Perth more."

There's a pause from Matt, and I can tell he's still trying to work out how to comfort a fellow artist.

"I hear what you're saying." He affirms again, so sincere and engaged. "Good nights don't make the shit ones easier."

"Yes!" I cry out, relieved he's put my thoughts into words. "It's like, what if the good ones were a fluke, and I'm actually fucking shit full time. And I'm wasting my time and my youth chasing some fucking dream that-"

"Holly." Matt interrupts, his voice soothing but firm. "It is a good show. You are fucking funny, and you deserve better crowds. This night doesn't prove shit. And you're not wasting a fucking thing."

I sit in his words for a few seconds, trying to hear them, trying to allow them to sink in.

"What if I am wasting my time, though?" I ask, ashamed to be so needy.

"So what?" Matt responds. "People waste their time getting shit faced and ruining your show, people waste their time watching movies, people waste their time writing poetry no one ever reads. Why does it matter?"

"Matthew..."

I can't think of anything else to say, unsure how to articulate that I appreciate his words, that I'm so thankful he didn't mind a late-night call, from the girlfriend who fucks off to tour some comedy show, in the hope of people seeing it.

I want to perform an interpretive dance, I want to launch into a Shakespearian monologue, I want to burst into song.

Anything to try and let him know that I love him.

Oh wow, I love him. I really do. Like, seriously. For real.

"Matthew, I- I love you." I say after who knows how long of a silence.

There's a moment, the seconds after I just go and say that, in which I wonder if it was the right thing to say. If I stuck my neck out for nothing. If I ruined a perfect moment somehow.

And I hear... laughter?

He's fucking laughing at me?

"Holly, you're amazing, you know that?" He chuckles. "Obviously I love you too, and of course this is how you say it for the first time."

Flight BA015

What do I do now?

I just sit here on this plane for the next twenty-one hours and think about how I've made this intense, cosmic connection?

I go back to my life, and she'll go back to hers, and we'll do what exactly?

A part of me feels that I've made a friend for life, that I've met my soulmate, the newest member of my family, someone so incredibly special.

Another part of me feels foolish. Falling for a married woman, what am I thinking?

Perhaps we can be friends, and that'll be enough?

But then, how often will we be talking, and I'll be staring at Rosa's lips? Thinking about holding her in my arms? Imagining trailing my arms up her back?

I can't think about that.

I'm not going to let myself wonder what could be, if things were just a little different, if the timing was ever so slightly changed, if we were very subtly edited characters.

If this were a novel, or a film, or a television series, it would be different.

If this was my teenage musings, the secret diary I kept hidden, right at the back of my wardrobe, oh, then it wouldn't end like this.

Here I was, thinking now I'm an adult and don't have to hide my queerness, I wouldn't have to pretend not to have feelings for other women. I could be loud, and proud, scream my feelings from a rooftop, then come down and kiss my girlfriend in the street.

But I guess it didn't work out that way.

And now I have to lust after a married woman. Or pretend not to. I can't even decide which is worse.

Twenty-one hours on a plane, and this is what I have to keep me occupied. Thoughts ripped right from the closeted teen I thought I'd left behind long ago, and a developing crush on someone I couldn't be more in sync with.

It's like I can read Rosa's mind. And her mine. As though we didn't have to verbalise a thing. But of course, we did. To check. Because we both like to check. And it's not some annoying thing to either one of us. Because we get it. And we get each other.

A chirpy flight attendant appears, I'm offered some coffee, and I remember the time Rosa and I went for coffee.

The little things bring me back. Always the little things.

It was only two weeks; how can I be this hung up? This isn't me. I'm not the person that thinks someone is my soulmate.

Soulmates are a statistical impossibility. I don't entertain impossibilities.

But I think about that coffee with her. Sitting in the Hackney vegan cafe that she'd raved about. Across from each other like a date.

And there was a moment.

Silent. Swift. Almost impossible to detect.

A moment in which I could almost be sure she felt it to.

I felt her looking at me, seeing me for who I really am. And I realised that no one had truly done that before. No one had really seen me before Rosa saw me.

Before she locked eyes with me over coffee, and something stirred in me.

Something real. New. Genuine. Beautiful in its simplicity.

A silent acknowledgment that we were both feeling a connection click into place and surge its power through our souls.

It served only to stab me square in the chest, reminding me that nothing could happen. Nothing.

Rosa had a wife, kids, a mortgage, and me? Well, I was leaving for Australia soon.

I was right back in that moment as I sipped my burnt and watery aeroplane coffee, staring blankly ahead, and trying my best not to cry.

Her face was so clear in my mind. Her voice. Her laugh. The way she stood. The way she dressed.

The way she spoke. Those words seemed animated, like they danced out of her mouth and waltzed their way into my brain.

And of course, I don't get her life, her choices. Little queer orphan that I am.

Most grown-ups do things more for others than themselves.

They grow up, get educated, get married, get a house, have a kid or two, work hard at their career, and they do almost all of it for others. For their parents, for their community, for the appearance of having things figured out.

They want to seem happy; they don't want anyone to worry about them, they want to seem like they're standing on their own two feet.

If something were to happen between Rosa and I, it would shatter all her facade-building she's poured so much of herself into.

And she's older, she's from a more traditional queer narrative. She fought for her right to marry her wife, for her right to have two children, for her right to be seen as just as settled as her straight brother.

Then there's me.

Arty, sexually driven, queer orphan. I cut my parents off before they could disown me. I let go of trying to make them proud long ago, when I realised it would never make me happy.

I'm not a forty-something who fought to be seen as 'normal'. I'm the next generation of queer.

I love and want to be loved without an endgame. I travel and explore. I change careers and postcodes. I have no intention of ever having what Rosa has.

I'm no one to think she'd ever actually consider it.

It would prove to the straights that we're all deviants. We're all broken and flighty and incapable of loving in a manner they deem acceptable and legitimate.

That's what such a deviation would prove. Rather than showing that a system of assumed long-term monogamy is harmful, and really just capitalist propaganda. Because a nuclear family with clear gender roles, yeah, that's the easiest way to buy and sell us.

So, I can't, I won't, I'm not going to imagine us together. To watch our moments together over and over again on this plane. Hoping that every re-watch helps to weave them into the very fibres of my brain.

I should just watch some movies, real ones, with people that aren't me. Use this time to escape my own existence. To distract myself with worlds that aren't my own, problems that don't concern me, characters I'll never meet.

Just allow all the noise to overtake me, to cradle me in its arms and take me away from thoughts of me and Rosa.

Rosa and me. The two of us.

It's not like there is any 'us' anyway.

It's either distraction or fixation, and I've got twenty-one hours to indulge one of them.

Fairy Lights

Brad lead my mum to the dance floor. Or, more accurately, the patio. Which to be fair, Auntie Grace had actually made very romantic with tealight lanterns and fairy lights.

She did always know how to throw a party.

Four hours in the car, a day of conversation with relatives that was either void of any real substance, or incessant arguing, that made me wish for the mind-numbing discussion of the weather, stuffing our faces cramped around tables.

And now the day's wound down, everyone's full and content, and it was Auntie Grace's idea to move out to the patio, as the balmy night approached.

I watched them slow dance, as the playlist Auntie Grace had created moved to 'Time After Time' by Cyndi Lauper.

And as the track played, mum and Brad looked at each other in a way I hadn't really seen before. They sang the words they knew, which was only a few, and smiled together with their whole bodies.

Most of the time when I'd seen them, they were both scrambling around the kitchen to shovel cereal into their faces, and throw coffee down their necks, trying to get to their jobs on time.

Which of course, was essentially the crack of dawn. Or 8am, same difference.

I'd stand bewildered for a few moments, before I'd think that maybe getting dressed, and coming back in fifteen minutes, would be a better idea than trying to wiggle in between them.

Though now, as Christmas Day winds down for another year, and the littlest kids watch TV in Auntie Grace's family room, while the adults dance or stand around and drink, and the young jaded almost-adults slump in lawn chairs and watch those adults, I see my mum and Brad for the first time.

I see their love, their tenderness.

They really do care about each other.

They look into each other's eyes and they glow. It shines out of them, orbits around them, shows anyone watching that they have something special.

Here I was thinking they were just two workaholics who'd happened to find each other, and Brad was some younger man trying to work through some mummy issues.

And who knows, maybe that was part of it, it's not my business either way. But it's been years now, and they clearly always had something real.

Mum rests her head on Brad's shoulder, as they hold each other close, shuffling back and forth. She smiles, a content, genuine smile. Not the kind she'd make on the phone to some client, while she was trying to seem like the most hard-working and accommodating lawyer on the planet.

No, this smile closed her eyes, filled her face, and radiated through her body.

He really did make her happy.

All I ever did was make sarcastic comments, and barely thank him for gifting me fifty dollars in a card for my birthday and Christmas. Every year.

I wasn't his kid. I wasn't his responsibility. I was part of the package with mum.

An only child in their teens, just what every thirty-two-year-old is looking for, to accompany a forty-five-year-old divorcee.

But he stepped in, he stepped up, and he was an ok step-dad.

While he was working more than full-time, doing more than half the work around the house, and making time to be all romantic with mum.

He'd kiss mum on the forehead, he'd cuddle up with her on the couch, he'd cook complicated meals on Sundays, just so he and mum could hang around the same kitchen they'd usually only rush through.

All I ever saw was some annoying dude trying to relate to me about my interests. And I reacted by giving him the cold shoulder, time after time.

But he stayed with my mum, and he still makes her smile. That's genuinely pretty special, I have to admit.

And here, from my plastic chair, I watch them swaying and shuffling, impaired by their alcohol consumption. Brad's still trying to sing the song to mum, and they still don't know the words, but they smile at each other anyway.

He gives her a kiss on the forehead, and says something that makes her bury her head in his chest.

I take another swig of my flavoured mineral water, as the sun sets on the scene of dancing lovers, at the end of a summertime Christmas.

Maybe I should walk over and tell Brad of my sudden revelations. Maybe I should find him at another time, and let him know I now understand I was a moody teenager, and I'm sorry.

Maybe he already knows.

Either way, those two are going to be alright. Maybe they always were.

Butterfly Wings

"I'm really sorry, Josie." August reiterates, his face tear-stained, the whites of his eyes growing red. "I can't keep pretending this is me."

I reach out a hand, a bridge over the troubled water between the hotel bed and my chair. August lifts his in response, and we meet in the middle, as we often did.

Not sure what to say in response, I let the quiet sit around us for a few moments, comfortable in the silence, as we often are.

"I really appreciate you talking this out with me." I cut through the silence, feeling a tear finally rolling down my cheek. "I mean it."

A squeeze from August lets me know he's heard me. Genuinely heard me.

"I just- I can't keep up anymore." August stammers out, his voice shaken by the emotion coursing through him. "I guess... I guess I didn't think I'd ever want to slow down. And now-now, it's like, like I feel myself getting so old some days, Josie."

Even with all we'd already talked out, everything August had already shared, these words really disarmed me.

I was getting older too.

But I really hadn't thought about how that had affected August, how being part of this touring lifestyle, being the Plus One to someone who's always on the move, had taken its toll.

We weren't kids fresh out of high school anymore, we weren't even young and stupid enough to not know better anymore, we were almost forty, and still living out of suitcases more often than not.

"And I- I don't want to hold you back." August pipes up, his voice still so uneven and strained. "I'd never want you to slow down because of me."

It sung, it knocked me off my feet, and kicked me while I lay there.

"A butterfly in hand." I blurt out, my voice smaller than expected, while I'm lost in thought and unfocused on anything in this hotel room.

"W-what...?" August asks, his voice shaking for two reasons.

"A butterfly in hand." I state again, our eyes meeting, his confusion evident. "If you- If you hold a butterfly too tightly, it'll die. You need to let it fly, that's why it has wings."

"I- I, yeah. Yeah." August stammers out, his face showing me the gears working behind the scenes. "That's why you have wings." He concludes.

That's us, finding our common ground, understanding each other despite our differences. Drifting apart despite wanting to stay together.

"That was one of my favourites. Such a good show." August reminisces, smiling through his tears.

"It was a tough tour though, remember the accommodation issues we had?" I add, recalling that year vividly.

"It was often something, wasn't it?" He laughs. "But whoa, that year had some big ones. And you won that award, well overdue."

He always was my cheerleader. Sitting with me while I read reviews, squeezing my hand through award ceremonies, talking me down when it all went to shit.

And that year, oh, taking 'A Butterfly In Hand' on the road was such a struggle. My first time bringing other performers with us, and the constant communication issues that resulted.

It really is easier to just work alone, and bring your partner along for the ride.

"Thank you, August." I chime in, realising something. "I never thanked you enough."

"You did, you said thank you all the time, in all types of ways." He replied, wiping the tears from his cheeks. "And you never had to. I was never there for a 'thank you', I was there to be by your side. If it was chatting to big timers or watching them on TV."

His words reached into my chest, and ripped my heart right out.

I'd felt stings of guilt here and there, now and then, brushing them off, thinking to myself that August actually got a pretty sweet deal, as my partner in life, and in the arts.

But to hear he didn't even care about that?

He didn't care about the fancy parties, mixing with the big names, being the dude with the kick-ass girlfriend?

He just wanted to be with me. Just me?

The whole acclaimed-theatre-maker-thing didn't sweeten the pot? That wasn't the big draw? It was just me?

"Josie?" He called me back into reality.

"Thank you, August." I reiterate.

"But you don't have to-"

I stood and pulled him into a hug, wrapping my limbs around his smaller frame, trying to tell him everything I was feeling, everything I wasn't ready to articulate with words, hoping it got through ok.

Breakfast

The smell of coffee, and the small stream of light peeking through the curtains, greeted me when I woke.

I looked around Jay's bedroom, taking in the mess we'd created.

Our clothes reaching each corner of a room Jay had cleaned before I arrived, keen to let me know he's a Good Boy. Because of course, Good Boys are rewarded kindly.

I slipped on my large t-shirt and my underwear, before finding the slippers Jay put out for me, and heading into his kitchen.

The housemate, Craig, was watching some action movie, zoned out on the couch. I gave a vague greeting, and he didn't respond.

Maybe he doesn't like hearing Jay making me cum again and again, then facing me the next morning. What a surprise. Who would ever think that someone wouldn't want to hear something like that? Completely baffling, am I right? The ladies in the back, you know what I'm talking about!

I walked past the sickeningly jealous Craig, and saw my Good Boy Jay cutting up fruit in the adjoining kitchen. He'd heard my greeting to Craig and was clearly hoping for his own.

"No 'good morning' for your Good Boy?" He asked playfully, feigning jealousy.

He smiled wide, and those full, luscious lips beckoned towards me. I leaned over the kitchen island, and gave him a chaste kiss.

"Good morning." I smiled. "My very Good Boy."

Jay bit his lip in response. And I raised an eyebrow playfully.

"I couldn't have you go hungry, Mistress." He teased, knowing full well how much Craig hates that Jay's a Needy Bottom.

"And I'm mildly impressed." I stated, noting Craig's exasperated groan at our words.

I moved around to stand behind Jay, while he divided the orange, apple, and peach pieces into two bowls.

Pushing myself against his body, I travelled my hands from the tops of his thighs, to his hips, over to his tummy. I did love that he's got that meat on his bones.

Folding myself around Jay, I lay my head in the nape of his neck, giving him a little bite on his traps.

That warranted a little whimper, and I was glad Jay wasn't holding a knife. I couldn't have my Good Boy hurting himself. That's my job.

Jay gripped the island as I pressed my body against his, reminding him of the way I pegged him with controlled intensity last night. I trailed my hand up to his nipples, ready to give him just a little tease, when something interrupted us.

"Can you guys tone it down?" Craig called from the couch, in a way that was not laced with any jealousy at all, not even the slightest ounce, you know what I'm saying, let me hear the ladies in the back!

"We're not 'guys', Craig. And gender is a spectrum, champ." Jay teases, as I pull back slightly, holding him in a way that was almost heterosexual.

"Uh! You know what I mean!" Craig protested, getting his pent-up arse off the couch and heading back to his room.

I pressed myself gently against Jay's butt, and he whimpered just in time for Craig to hear it, before he slammed his door like the fifteen-year-old boy he still is.

As I stepped back to allow him just enough space, Jay whipped around to face me. I stroked his beautiful face, admiring its strong, defined features.

He was beauty personified. Those plump lips, that bold nose, those almond eyes, that glorious black skin. I could stare at him all day.

I moved my hand around to rub his shaved head, I loved the sensation, and he loved a head massage. He closed his eyes, and a soft smile played along those kissable lips. And for a moment, we stayed there, enjoying the pleasure and connection of intimate touch.

Abruptly, I stopped massaging Jay's head and quickly gave him a slap on that round arse.

"I thought you said you weren't going to let me go hungry?!" I interjected, with fake outrage.

"Of course, Mistress Mikoto!" Jay replied, with genuine enthusiasm. "Please, have a seat."

Jay lead me two steps to the small kitchen table, where a cafetière, two cups, and two plates waited for me.

He pulled out my chair, I moved to sit, and he pushed that chair back in. Giving me a little kiss on the part in my short bob.

It was one of the only styles that works with my thick, Asian hair. Not that this fact in any way shut up my relatives, and their comments of how 'modern' my hairstyle was, with clear traditional disapproval in their voices.

But they're trying to hold onto a culture they see disappearing before their very eyes, in the form of my very hair, so I try to cut them some slack.

I watched Jay bring our fruit salads to the table, along with fresh bread, topped with some hummus and sliced tomatoes. He knows me so well.

"Is the spread to your liking, Mistress?" Jay asked of me, sitting down beside me.

His face was pleading for my approval, and urgh, how I loved that.

I made a short show of looking around the small table, noting the place settings, the precision with which Jay had cut the fruit, the care with which he'd plated the bread and hummus, which was clearly from the Turkish shop down the street, and not the big supermarket.

"I'm... very pleased." I stated plainly, my face still hard, showing just a little bit of gratification.

"Thank you, Mistress." Jay replied, averting his eyes, and looking into his lap.

I reached over and gave his thigh a squeeze.

"You don't need to check if your hard dick is obvious." I teased. "I could tell you're getting hard just by looking at your face."

"But I don't need to know!" Craig cried out. I guess he'd thought this was an opportune time to re-emerged from his room.

"Don't worry, Craig." Jay teased. "I'm sure there's plenty of people who'd like to control your orgasms."

"URGH!" Craig objected. "You two are fucking disgusting!"

I guess at least he remembered gender is a spectrum, and dropped the 'guys' this time.

Baby steps.

Soaps And Hot Lunches

My grandmother must have been so lonely once I left, and I had no idea.

Gone for days, blank behind the eyes, busying herself with the funeral arrangements and taking care of me.

I would mostly just sit and watch her, unaware of what to do, unable to understand her loss, physically present, but essentially useless.

Company. Another human being in the house that used to have a husband.

And I guess I was the eight-year-old stand-in husband. Standing in at my mother's instruction. For that week at least.

So, we'd watch her stories together, she'd cook a hot lunch, dinner was toast or cereal, she'd answer calls about flowers and coffins and payments.

Those days were a blur for me, but no doubt trudging along for her.

Dragging and painful.

I tried to do my part. Washed the dishes, helped with hanging out clothing and linens, tried not to get in the way as best I could.

A child and a grandmother. A few days together. A funeral at the end.

That day was the strangest of all.

An early morning.

Sat up at the dining table. Preparing sandwiches, cheese, and biscuits, for the wake. The sun barely risen, the house absolutely freezing, my young body weary at the ungodly hour, just the two of us.

A car ride with my cousins.

My grandmother far quieter than she'd been these past few days. Nothing else to plan, no more chores with some eight-year-old asking questions and making jokes. Just a car ride to bury her husband.

A modern church.

One with all that new architecture, like a slick town hall, none of those bleeding paintings of Jesus; just beige walls, large windows, and a podium on a stage, behind a dead man in a box.

My mother had brought something for me to wear, I didn't like it, but it seemed silly to complain. It wasn't my husband in that box, so maybe I should just do what I'm told, and not make this day any worse.

My cousin who drove us, the one who had twenty years on me, spoke about the man we were all here to say goodbye to. Wearing a tan suit and a white shirt, no tie, like a beach-bound James Bond. He mentioned the light colour was for my grandfather, who stated on many occasions, that he hated people wearing black to funerals.

I looked down to my royal blue and cream ensemble, and I liked it a little more.

There were so many faces I didn't know, people I never met who swore they knew me as a baby, and wanted to bask in the fact I was a baby no longer.

Most of them didn't attend the wake, they only came for the ceremony. They didn't come back to my grandmother's house, where she unwrapped the sandwiches, cheese, and biscuits, we'd prepared that earlier that morning, and lay them out on her coffee table.

It was cramped in her house; the structure wasn't built for even the small number of immediate family who had made their way to the wake.

So many of them said the same phrases, like dialogue from a script I'd never read, while looking at me with a strange expression I didn't understand.

In return, I nodded, and feigned a small smile, hoping the interaction would be over soon. It worked with every one of them.

As the mid-morning turned to afternoon, my mother informed me I'd be going home with her today, and I should pack my things.

And I went home, went back to school, went back to what I knew as normal, but my grandmother had nothing of the sort to return to.

I was only a child then, not really old enough to understand much of that week, but when I look back on that particular day now, I think only of that night.

My grandmother's night.

An old woman watching her stories alone, cleaning dishes alone, crawling into bed alone.

Dinner Date

"Professor Dork!" I call from the kitchen, hearing the door unlock and close softly.

Pausing my 'Femme Power' playlist, I hear no response, only the shuffling sound of shoes coming off, being placed in the rack, and a coat and bag being hung up.

"George?" I call again, with a sprinkle of concern.

No answer.

Then, I hear it.

I turn the stove off, and wipe my tomato-slick hands on the tea towel over my shoulder.

When I see George, I see my guess was right.

He leans against the door with one hand, covers his face with the other, sobbing so softly, I almost can't hear him. But of course, I didn't need to hear to know.

"...George..."

I reach out to my date, guiding his hand away from his face. His eyes are already red, and his cheeks flushed.

George avoids my gaze, as I step a little closer, offering to take him into my arms.

He responds by crumbling to his knees, and wrapping his arms around my hips, burying his head into my tummy.

I stroke his hair and rub his back. After a moment or two, I slow to a halt, and hold him there.

The muffled sound of George's wails and his heaving body fills the silence of my flat, everything else remains motionless and quiet, even the pasta on the stove is still.

It seems the time stretches and glues us to our spots, as little by little, George settles. His breathing begins to steady, his wailing dulls to a low sniffle, he lets go.

"...Sorry, I'm all snotty..." George sheepishly mentions.

I let out a short laugh. It cuts through the screaming silence in a stark contrast to George's words, which merely floated.

George laughs a little too.

"You can get snot on my jumper any day, Georgey Boy." I comfort, stroking his hair once again.

"Do you... have a...?" George asks, pulling back slightly to show his tear-stained face and runny nose.

I look around and see the tissues are too far to reach.

"Here." I declare, whipping the towel from my shoulder, and handing it to George.

He hesitates.

"That's what washing machines are for, you dork." I reassure.

George takes the hand towel, and drops the rest of the way to the floor. He dabs his eyes, and blows his nose in a way I can tell is him trying not to be too loud about it.

I join him on the floor, and run the back of my hand up and down his face, as he avoids my gaze a second time.

"Oh, sorry..." He coyly remarks, dabbing my jumper with the hand towel.

I steady his hand, as he tries to dry his tears from my clothes, and George looks further away from me.

Taking the towel from him, I sit cross-legged and gesture for George to settle into my lap.

He responds, laying his head down and wrapping his hands around my thigh.

I begin to slowly stroke his hair, humming odd bits of tunes I know, trying to fill the space with some sound.

It seems that the flat falls away, that we're occupying a vast, endless space, in which no one else exists, and nothing else has ever happened.

We stay in our nothingness and everythingness for who knows how long. George holding my thigh, me running my fingers through his hair, us... being.

"The voices won't go away, Maya. They won't..." George mumbles, breaking the silence.

"I know, Georgey."

And I did. And he knew I did.

"I'm sorry. I didn't mean to ruin our date night, I-"

"George." I reassure. "You didn't ruin anything. You're fighting to shut the voices up. It's not an easy fight, and you're doing so well."

"But... you cooked, and I barrelled in and-"

"You're doing so well."

"But, I-"

"You are doing so well."

"B-but..."

Silent tears began to weave their way down George's face. I wipe them away, and he takes my hand, and squeezes it.

"It's not a burden for you to have a hard time." I comfort.

George squeezes.

"You're not broken. You're not selfish. You're a human being."

George folds himself up and moves away from me, I can only see half of his face. I stay put, not sure if he needs space or not.

"I'm not angry at you, you haven't disappointed me."

George lets out a short wail.

"I love you, George."

He hides his face from me completely.

I move a hand across the floor, reaching out to him slowly.

He feels my movement.

"Can you hold me, Maya?"

"Of course."

I move myself over to George, slowly standing.

"On the couch?" I ask, holding my hand out.

"Ok."

George takes my hand, and little by little, comes to his feet. I guide him the few steps to the couch, and help him to settle into the sofa, wrapping myself all around him.

The silence falls once more, and we fall into it.

Cake Plate

I push around my cake, having only consumed a bite or two of the Black Forest gâteau. And honestly? I don't know what I'm hoping will happen if I keep busy with this plate.

Maybe I'm hoping I won't look like such a stupid fucking loser who let the best thing that ever happened to me walk out of my life.

Maybe I'm hoping it'll stop me from looking up at her, on that huge table, with those in-laws on either side, and her fresh husband next to her.

What am I supposed to do now?

I can't get drunk.

No one wants some drunk dude at his ex's wedding causing a scene.

And besides, I'm two years sober. And I'm sure everyone here knows how important that is to me.

I do.

I do, damn. She said that, and now she's married. Genuinely married. Tied the fucking knot and now I'm the pathetic ex, in his dead dad's tux, at her damn wedding.

Or am I the progressive, enlightened guy, who's mature enough to support an old friend?

Either way, I'm just staring into a whipped cream-covered plate, cutting cake into smaller and smaller pieces. Afraid to look up for too long, because of what I might see.

I was just watching her commit to someone else.

A couple of hours ago, she stood up in front of her family, his family, and so many friends, relatives, and I guess me as well, and she told them that he's the one for her.

She told them how happy he makes her. How much he supports and loves her, how much he's there for her.

That wasn't me.

I tried, but it wasn't me. She was too good for me. I always knew it. And I guess I hoped it would take her a little longer to realise.

I had my own baggage that I wasn't owning up to. I wasn't there for her enough. I was drowning myself in alcohol every weekend. And she was the one who drove me to those A.A. meetings.

Sure, loss does some shit to you, but I shouldn't have taken it out on her like that. It was my dad that went and fucking died. And she was the one who tried to talk to me about it.

She was patient, she was funny, she was fucking there. And I wasn't, I checked right out.

Those times when we'd just watch shitty movies and she'd riff about the dialogue, just to make me smile, that was it for sure.

Those were some of the best nights of my life.

So, what did I do? I fucked it up.

And I'm better now, but it's too late. If I was her, I wouldn't give me another chance.

She deserves that dude.

He's all nice and everything. I've seen them at the supermarket getting all that healthy stuff. He takes care of his body and mind, they get out in nature, talk about their feelings and all that.

She lights up when she looks at him.

I bet he doesn't get fucking black out drunk on date night and sleep through the whole next day, ignoring all her texts and calls.

She thought of me all the time. Kept checking in and trying to connect.

And most of the time, I couldn't even text her back for hours and hours.

The fact she even invited me. The fact she wanted to clear the air before today. The fact she introduced me to heaps of these people, and I went and sat by myself and pushed my cake around.

Always way too good for me.

Always the bigger person.

Caring and intelligent, charismatic and hilarious, beautiful and kind.

Always.

All I could do was sit stony faced as they had their first dance to 'You Really Got Me' by The Kinks. It was a killer choice, and they had fun with it, but I'm too up my own arse to swallow my pride and crack a smile for a two-minute moment.

They were happy, dancing, sharing their day of commitment with people they care about. Throwing a free damn party and inviting a dead-beat piece of shit like me.

I just sat there during that first dance, and I'm sitting here now.

I brace myself and look up. Oh no. She's spotted me. She's walking over. And look, she's glowing and genuinely cares. Fuck.

"Do you wanna come dance, sillyface?" Alice asks, her eyes kind and warm, the scent of vanilla surrounding her, inviting and comforting.

Using the pet name she gave me, to boot. She remembers.

"Ahhh. It's ok. I'm still enjoying my cake." I reply, managing to put the tiniest bit of pep into my voice. "It was a beautiful ceremony. And Gumede's a super sweet guy."

I hoped it sounded sincere. I didn't want to fuck up her special day.

"If you keep 'enjoying' that cake, you're gonna split the atom, Mr. Fission." She retorted, pointing at my plate of near-crumbs.

She always was ready with a joke. Always trying to lighten the mood and make everyone feel at ease.

I laughed. She laughed. It was almost like it had been.

Or could've been.

"Come on, James." She encouraged. "One dance. It'll only take a few minutes. Then you can finish your important work here, Science Guy."

Alice held her hand out, smiling at me like I genuinely mattered. Like I hadn't broken her heart five years ago. Like she still saw something worth saving in me.

I stood up, brushing some crumbs off my dad's tux, and took her hand.

We moved to the dance floor and I realised which song was playing. You've got to be fucking kidding me.

Aerosmith's 'Don't Wanna Miss A Thing'. Shoot me down where I almost stand.

"We can wait for a different song." I said, pulling back slightly.

"I requested it, sillyface!" Alice retorted. "I haven't forgotten."

She hasn't forgotten.

All these years and she hasn't forgotten. Gumede is the luckiest man on the planet. But luck has nothing to do with it.

He's a loving person. A great person. Not withdrawn and broken like me.

I can't believe she hasn't forgotten. I couldn't listen to this song for years after we broke up. And here we were, about to dance to it.

"Is it ok if I take your waist?" I ask, reaching out tentatively.

"James! I'm married, not a nun." She shot back, laughing, placing my hand on her purple gown. "And you're... you know, you're sillyface."

She smiled softly. And we slow danced. Respectfully, of course, leaving room for the holy spirit and all that.

She'd remembered this song only made sense once I met her. She'd remembered that I'd been embarrassed to like such a sappy song at first, and she'd teased me about being embarrassed.

And I'd ended up singing that song to her while I held her. I'd kiss her shoulders and stroke her arm.

Before things went down the toilet. Before I let them.

But fuck it, here we were, some seven years after that song first made sense to me, dancing to it at her wedding.

Alice had requested the song, because she knew what it meant to me. To us. And she'd got me off my self-loathing arse to have one moment with me and this song.

I started tearing up. I looked down, hoping Alice wouldn't see.

I knew on some new-wave, super-enlightened level it was ok. It was ok to be a dude with feelings. And to let those out. To cry because an old friend still wanted me to feel happy.

"James, you can cry." Alice reassured, ducking and weaving, trying to catch my eye.

It was like someone had opened the flood gates. And suddenly I had tears streaming down my face.

All the time I spent hating myself for what I'd done to Alice; and she'd gone and dealt with that, moved on, taken care of herself, and found someone to treat her right.

And in among all that, she'd reached out to me, and tried to make me feel a little bit of that joy.

She really was too good for me.

Yielded Growth

"Yeah, so it's like, I'm thinking, what are we gonna do, as this dickhead's venue, you know?"

Nameless Comedy Producer's words faded out into a crowded, indistinguishable, wall of noise, as the scene around me fell into an unfocused haze.

The mix of other characters huddled around the table in this almost-empty bar, were like a Greatest Hits, or in this case Greatest Flops, of everything I'd been avoiding for so long.

There was those listening, those actively looking to butt in with some witty one-liner, and those actively not listening, all as Nameless Comedy Producer continued her story of The Great Venue Debacle of 2019.

It was all too familiar in times past, but now, all too alien.

Years ago, I'd sat around many tables like this, waiting and hoping to be able to jump in with a funny line. Constantly trying to one-up everyone around me. And if I could, surely then, I'd come out as the Victor Of All Other Comedians.

I thought it was of the upmost importance to impress, hoped it would mean I'd be welcomed in. Hoped that I'd be part of something.

But I didn't stop to ask if I even wanted to be One Of The Comics.

Then wouldn't you know: I didn't.

I was looking for community and acceptance in all the wrong places.

Time passed, and I knew I had grown, but not exactly how much.

It's such an incredibly difficult concept to measure: growth. There's no scale, there's no litmus test, no wise and aged secondary character letting you know you've outgrown your younger self.

No, it's something you find in moments least expected.

I'd only thought I should get out of the house, head to a comedy night I used to frequent a few years ago, maybe catch up with some old and new faces.

Hit the town, be social, why not, right?

But now, I'm hit with the realisation of just how much I've outgrown these types.

I don't want to impress them, I'm not trying to one up anyone, I'm not going home wondering if I'll lose gigs because I wasn't laughing hard enough at someone's sub-par quip.

Every joke I made was to feel a sense of connection, but that connection was so often missed and fruitless.

It was like speaking different languages.

It was screaming into the night in an empty town.

It was trying to catch someone's eye to let them know they've dropped something, but they never see you, and even with an attempt to call after them, they disappear into the crowd never having known you were trying to help.

As Nameless Comedy Producer completed the Tale Of Dickhead Comics At Her Venue, another face at the table jumped in with a story of their own.

Interchangeable Open Mic Comic began to weave his tale, and I could feel everyone itch with attempts to again cut in with supposedly hilarious retorts, so hollow and relentless.

This is it. This is why everyone is huddled around a bar table on a Monday evening, at half an hour to midnight.

It does seem, trying to make the best joke during someone else's story, is somehow the best The Table Crew can hope for, even when there's so much more outside that frosted window.

It's somehow all pressing and interesting enough to hang on after a gig, after all their day jobs, on the first day of a five-day working week.

And all of that is either not as exhausting for them, as it is for me, or it's peppered with enough substances to be... **fun** for them?

Constantly looking to reply, rather than to listen, that's the peak of the human experience here?

I can't pinpoint when I made the switch, but there was a moment when I stopped always looking for a punchline, and instead began looking to understand whomever I was speaking with.

Maybe it was the realisation that there was no real affinity in humour. It was a fleeting closeness, an opening of a door, but not a building of a home.

It could have been all the conversations spent diving into someone's beautiful mind, the many discussions flavoured with a mutual curiosity and respect, the mountains of heart-to-hearts that broadened my perspective and showed me a side of myself I didn't even know existed.

Who could've thought that ten people all trying to out-joke each other couldn't even begin to compare to all that?

I reached for my jacket, and clearly it caught The Bar Gaggle by surprise, as I'm guessing someone was either attempting to share some surface tale or someone else was attempting to jut in.

The group looked at me with a mix of confusion and contempt, as they collectively realised, I hadn't been listening for some time, and in turn, gave absolutely no clout to anything any of them had to say.

Not to mention the fact I gave no weight to any of their abilities to book me, or not book me, at their venues, for their gigs, or to future hollow chinwags.

"Cool to catch up, I'm heading out." I announced as I pushed out my chair and some of them clambered to stand up and I'm guessing, give me some sort of goodbye gesture. "Nah, I've gotta leave."

And with that, a stunned and awkward atmosphere thickened, as I grabbed the strap of my backpack and headed out into the crisp Melbourne evening. Their shocked chattering hanging in the air.

The fresh and frozen night air hugged me as I made my way down the laneway and toward the tram two streets down. I took in a deep breath and reassured myself I didn't owe anyone in that pub a thing, and most of all, not my precious time on this beautiful winter night.

I fished for my headphones in my backpack, and donned them, deciding to play something that reminded me of a great love.

As I reached the tram stop, and sat on the freezing metal seat, I took in the night cityscape, as the solemn sounds filled my ears. And soon, memories of better conversations will replace the loop of scenes from The Bar Gang.

ScotRail

The 15:30 to London Kings Cross. Suitcase in the luggage compartment. Backpack in the overhead storage. Headphones on.

I slump down into my assigned seat, stare out the window at Edinburgh Waverly, and wait for this train to depart.

It had seemed so good. Such a good fit. Something that should have worked out.

On paper.

In theory.

Not in practice with real feelings involved.

Soon enough, I'll be watching the Scottish countryside go by, and there'll be rich greenery to occupy my wandering eyes. But for now, it's just the other people boarding this train, and the reminder that life just goes on.

Maybe they're going somewhere interesting, the other passengers. Maybe their lives are changing. Maybe they've also just broke up a deflated relationship.

I still loved Daniel. The timing was just... not right. Not now.

Playing back that final goodbye, I wondered if it could've gone better. Differently. Somehow.

I'd gone into the living room, where Daniel was hiding himself away. He lay on the couch, wrapped in a blanket, despite the fact he always ran hot. I'd called out, he'd sat up, smiled in a way that was supposed to be encouraging. I'd approached, and we'd had a strange, performative hug.

He'd offered to help with my bags, and as usual, he knew I didn't actually want or need any help, he was just trying to be useful. Helpful. Loving.

So, we'd awkwardly moved the bags down the two flights of stairs, from the flat we were supposed to be living in together, and I'd walked to Waverly.

Now, lucky me had four hours to think about all of this, and the train is only just leaving the station.

I hadn't thought it was going to last forever. That's not how relationships work. They bloom, they have conflicts, sometimes the conflicts can be resolved, sometimes they can't, and they end. That's it.

The feeling changed, and although I did think, or more likely hoped, those feelings could come back, Daniel wasn't so sure.

And these things only work if both people are into it. Or so I've heard.

For hours, we sat on opposing sides of that lounge room, a room which had become Daniel's way of escaping me. Hours and hours of talking, and avoiding eye contact, and saying what we were really feeling.

It hurt. It punched me in the gut to think I could've been so blind. That I could've been hoping so hard, I saw something that wasn't there. Or didn't see something that was there.

At least we got it all out in the open. At least neither of us yelled, or threw things, or attacked the other. We were mature and communicative about it. That was worth something, in its own way.

Maybe not in a way that mattered right now. When it was so fresh. Stinging and exposed. Though perhaps in a few weeks, or months, or years, it'll matter.

I keep going back to so many moments when I didn't see it. I didn't notice Daniel pulling away, distancing himself, shutting me out.

I took him at his word so many times. Let things slide three, four, ten times. Ignored tiny, silent, desperate signs.

It wasn't until I started to feel it too. Until I started to pull away, that I even noticed things had been slowly deteriorating between us.

Only when it affected me did I even see it.

I was too self-concerned to even care. To even check in. To talk. Until all the foundations had already fallen.

And with so much pressure on both of us, I hoped that was it all it was.

The pressure of finding somewhere to live, the steps we were both taking to work through our shitty childhoods, along with trying to pay bills and just fucking stay alive.

But, at some point, it wasn't about any of that. It was about us. About us not being in love.

Someone who is more emotionally intelligent, might say I should feel sad. Or feel something at least. Anything at all.

All I feel is numb. Going through the motions. Getting through the day. Like I'd been doing recently with Daniel.

But I've also cried my tears. There with Daniel in that living room.

So maybe I'm not a psychopath for not feeling anything now? What else is there to feel? To explore? To express?

There were too many moments, in which he'd hurt me, swirling around my brain, to be heartbroken about a shell of a relationship ending well past it's use-by-date.

The time he told me I'd '"already said" that I was so happy to be with him, I'd stopped listening to my whiny emo songs.

The point I noticed he stopped occasionally looking over at me while he was working away on his laptop, and I was pottering away on mine.

The moment I'd come home and discovered he'd moved into the lounge room, so he didn't have to sleep next to me.

At the beginning, I remember singing songs I never liked before, noticed him always catching a peek of me while he'd type away, felt him always reaching out for me in our shared bed.

But those memories were tarnished now.

Maybe each of us was hoping the other was going to say something first. It could've saved both of us some time.

I suppose the best I can hope for is one day, maybe a year from now, we can catch up like old friends.

Who knows, maybe I'll even end up being some huge part of his life.

Right now, I'm going to enjoy watching the countryside go by, and listening to my whiny emo songs.

Railings

A chair turned away from me.

A man in that chair.

A TV lighting the dark room.

I watch him from the landing, my head pressed up to the railing. The wood is neither warm nor cold, the carpet itches the skin on my knees. My dress doesn't cover them. It's too hot to wear trousers today.

A metallic sound tells me he's finished another beer, as it joins the others on the floor, the TV light playing off its curves.

Another familiar sound as a new can is opened and a sip is taken. The burp rings out through the empty lounge room, even over the sounds of the TV.

He's fascinating to me, this man that never sits with the rest of us. Never spends time with me, with my siblings, with my mother.

He gets up, goes to work, comes home, takes over the living room, sits in front of the TV, the sun sets, he opens can after can, and he stays there.

Never turning on the lights around him, choosing instead to sit in the darkness and drink alone.

It's the same every day, even on the weekends. Sure, work is replaced with outings with other men, sometimes fishing, sometimes the dog races, sometimes the pub, but it's all the same really.

The man goes where he wants, comes back, and he sits there.

He doesn't join us for dinner. He doesn't come with us to get groceries. He never picks me up from anything. He hardly ever speaks a single word to me, or anyone else in this house.

He's the odd one out, sitting down there rather than with us. Watching TV rather than sharing a meal with his family. Spending his days with strangers rather than me.

A big part of me wants to know him, learn his secrets, hear about his life.

But I don't, I can't, I'm not allowed.

He's a distant, shadowy figure, completely anonymous to me.

The others know him. Or knew him.

My siblings tell me he wasn't always like this, that I'm just too young to remember how he used to be.

My mother talks of him before the children, of his hobbies, his skills, his interests, things I've never heard from the man himself.

Apparently, he had a whole life before we came along. He was a completely different person. He has reasons for acting the way he does.

None of it actually explains him to me, none of it makes him seem any more familiar, or makes him even seem like a person.

They're only stories, they're not real to me. They could be made up; they could've never happened for all I know.

So, I watch him from the landing, I try to know him on his terms.

But soon the carpet will itch too much, I'll get sweaty behind my knees, my face will grow sore from being pushed up against the railing. And so, I'll get up from my lookout spot.

I'll get up and go do something else, go write in my notebook, go join my siblings, go play a video game, whatever seems fun at the time.

I'll have grown tired of trying to know him for that day, it gets boring after a while.

And one day, I'll get up and never sit down in my lookout spot again.

Xenolith

The twisting in my stomach. The longing for just another taste of your presence. The sense that memories are all we'll ever have. The anger and frustration at this being over before it began.

Do you feel that too? Or am I losing touch with reality?

I've never been one to be particularly grounded, or tethered to the physical realm.

You held me down, though. Not like a lead balloon, or an unstoppable force meeting an immovable object. No. Like an anchor. An anchor and a compass, and the whole damn ship.

I stood on the bow, and you watched on. Never needing to reach out and pull me back, but present, ready to grab my wrist should I begin to fall.

The wind cut through my hair and the icy flecks stung my face, and you didn't try to tell me to step back, to come inside and warm up.

You enjoyed my delight in the sensations, in taking in the beautiful view. The black, frozen night, surrounding my lone presence on that bow.

I fell into the nothingness of it all. Saturated myself in the endless, boundless, blistering cold of the horizon.

The sea and the sky meeting somewhere in the distance, but I'd never see it. And neither would you.

We'd simply float on our ship.

Me, pushing myself as far out to the edge as I ever could. And you, a few paces behind. With just enough trepidation for the both of us to stay alive.

That moment would exist forever, and never exist at all.

It would be everything between us.

A scene. A moment. A blip in time that hopefully, we could carry with us until the end of our days.

Or not.

Maybe this was never an icy night on a ship for you.

Maybe it was merely a perfectly pleasant meet-cute on an extraordinarily ordinary day.

Nothing to report home about, but a sweet moment, nonetheless.

Maybe it's something you wouldn't remember at first.

A story buried deep in your mind. Something you'd be able to pull back into focus, after a sharp turn, and a backstreet detour.

And you'd see it. It'd be true in your mind's eye for just long enough to bring a short, kind, friendly smile.

You'd look off to the distance for a split second, absorb yourself back into the memory, and breathe into it. Then, quickly snap back into this world, and nothing will have changed.

The memory would sprinkle a warmth on your soul, and be gone. Disappear into that back-catalogue of almost-forgettable interactions. It was after all, nothing to phone home about. Perhaps.

Or perhaps not.

Perhaps you also felt the collision of glorious hope and destructive despair. The sense that neither of us would be the same again. We'd carry each other with us. Occasionally wondering where the other is, what they're doing, if they've thought of us recently.

And who's to say we'd ever actually be unhappy? Who can assert we'd be empty and unfulfilled? Who's to suggest we'd walk around feeling a slight itch that could never be scratched?

Am I far too romantic to think of life this way? A naive hope that a true, deep, fulfilling happiness can be found, even if only for a moment.

A brief, life-affirming scene that would play over and over until the end of my days.

Am I too idealistic? To think of us against the world as some beautiful crusade, something that will give us a purpose and passion unparalleled in our other experiences.

Or am I just selfish? Looking for something in you that was never truly there. Reading into your words, and looking into your glances, projecting onto your presence. Seeing what I want to see, then demanding the world bend to my whims and give me what I crave.

I would never blame you for resenting me. For wishing from time to time that I did hold back just a little. For pulling you from a slumber in which you were perfectly comfortable. For telling you I felt the same and injecting poison into your life.

If you resented me, it would be so much easier to feel less guilty.

I want to hate you. Then, I want to be indifferent towards you. And then, I want you to be that distant, but pleasant, meet-cute on an ordinary day.

And I hope it will start with the resentment that I don't yet feel. Instead of the anger and pain that I was stupid enough to fall for you.

You were so kind and loving, and I took that from you, and you gave me more, and I gave it back, and we spun and spun and we fell into the blindingly white void together.

Too bright to look directly into, so we looked into each other.

And I can't speak for you, but I loved what I saw. What you showed me. What you allowed me to see of you. The truths you told, the hurt you shared, the jokes we made.

So, I have to feel something awful towards you, and hope that it replaces all the good. All the highs and the happiness. The delight that came with our conversations. The light I'd feel when I spoke about you to others. The bashfulness I'd feel when I'd reminisce over photos of us.

It's all too positive. It hurts too much. It cuts too deep.

It's not like the icy winds of our ship's bow. It's a slice of the flesh, without the catharsis. The burst appendix, that can't be ripped from my abdomen.

It hangs around after it's welcome, winding and twisting inside me. But it's nothing like real pain. It doesn't have a start and end. It doesn't provide any relief, any sense of reason. It just burrows and eats its way further and further, and just when I think it's starting to leave me, it comes back in, wave after wave.

Relentless, unquenchable, unparalleled. The Dripping Water Torture of love.

If only the droplets would stop falling, if only leaving my body, and travelling back to our frozen ship would provide some respite. If only forgetting about you was permanent, and it was possible to recolour those conversations. If you'd just say something, do something, to make me hate you.

Then our ship would be swept up in a storm, whose powerful nature has never before been documented. An arctic, relentless, swirl of the coldest water and the most burning of lightning.

It would be destroyed, and so would we.

And I'd be done. You'd be done.

Our lives would be our own again.

Interrogation

Securing the orange necktie around Hugh's wrists, I stand behind him, and trace the back of my hands up to his shoulders, then run my palms down his chest.

A whimper escapes his parted lips.

I pull his head back roughly, and bring him into an upside-down kiss. Passionate. Forceful. A little bite at the end.

Then shove his head forward. A sharp exhale, and he stays there, as he always does. My word, he looks good. Tied to a chair like that.

"Thank you, Ms. Menchit." He breathes.

I smirk, but of course, he can't see me.

"Mmmm, ever the polite boy." I affirm.

"Of course, Ma'am."

I reach for my riding crop, and it seems he's heard that.

Standing in front of him, his eagerness is palpable. I do love to see it.

I draw a line with the crop, from his foot, to his knee, across his thigh, pressing briefly on his crotch, up his chest, to his blind-folded face.

Pulling back the tiniest amount, I give him a gentle little tap on the cheek.

An impatient moan.

I hold the crop high above my head, it makes the most delightful whip as it goes slicing through the air, then it makes contact with his thighs, giving a loud smack.

A sharp, deep moan.

"Thank you. One." He breathes.

"Good boy." I praise.

A whimper.

"May I have another, please, Ms. Menchit?"

"I don't know." I muse, grabbing his face sharply, holding his lips an inch from mine. "You have been good, I guess... but your manners right now could be... improved."

A pleading moan.

"Please, Ms. Menchit, I'd love another. I want it, please."

"You... want it?"

I let go of his face and stand over him.

"I need it, Ma'am. Please, please, I need to feel your power. I need you, please. Please!"

Smack. Inhale. Moan.

"Thank you. Thank you, Ma'am. You're so good to me. Two."

Whimper. Smack. Groan.

"Thank you, thank you, thank you. Three."

I drop the crop and sit on Hugh's lap. Whimper.

My hands are on his upper thighs. They're rubbing, pushing, pulling, as I hold my face ever so closely to his. Feeling the desperation and arousal dripping off him.

I push down on those thighs, and stand up, keeping my mouth a breath from his. I nudge him softly, brushing my lips just a little against his. A pleading moan.

One of my hands makes its way up to his face, grabbing and pinching all the way, taking note of the delicious reactions his over-eager body yields.

Cradling his face in one hand, rubbing my thumb back and forth over his cheek, I take one big step back.

"Beg me for it." I demand.

A strained whimper.

"Please, please, I need you to slap me Ms."

"Again!"

"Please, Ma'am. Please!"

"AGAIN!"

"I want you to hurt me, please. PLEASE!"

Smack. A gut-punch groan.

I place my hand on his shoulder, and bring my arm back.

Thud. A proper gut-punch groan.

"T-thank yo-you, Ma'am. T-than-"

I interrupt Hugh's stuttered words with a kiss, sitting on his lap once more, surrounding him, holding him there. Taking all his sexual energy in, drinking in his pleasure and pain, his need to be pushed around and humiliated. Exquisite.

Pulling back, I trail kisses from his cheek, to his neck, and unbutton his shirt just enough to place a few kisses on his collar bone.

He utters 'thank you' a thousand times, as he lets out beautiful sounds and his body responds to my touch in the most enticing way.

In one swift move, I stand over him again, holding onto his shoulders, so he knows exactly where I am. I nudge his knee with mine, then trail it up his thigh.

"Oh... oh, please, please, please, Ma'am. I need it, please."

I press gently at first, then lay my full weight into his crotch.

A stuttered low groan.

I pull back, breaking all contact. A pleading whimper.

As I walk around to stand behind him, the anticipation in his strained breathing is delightful.

I bring one hand up to his head, slowly drawing circles through his hair. Gentle, tactile, a short respite.

A soft low moan.

I move the circles down, reaching the back of his neck, and moving around to his throat. I trail soft touches up and down that throat for a moment, maybe two.

His breathing becomes more and more uneven and desperate with each stroke.

"Ma'am... please, pl-"

I shut him up with a sharp grab of that throat. I do wish I could see his eyes behind that blindfold, they're rolling back, no doubt. I guess I'll just have to imagine.

Three... four... five... I release him with one swift motion, pushing his head down, as he gasps for air.

I hold his head in both hands, and lay a kiss on the crown while he breaths his thanks countless times in between pants.

After a moment of rest, I slip his blindfold off, throw it to some corner, and move around to face him.

Hugh's cheeks are flushed, his breathing stilted and needy, his eyes wet with tiny tears forming at the corners, he looks gorgeous.

He looks up at me, like he'd do absolutely anything I'd ask, and it makes me want to give him everything he'd ask for.

But of course, I can't just go and do it, what would be the fun in that?

I softly run the back of my hand up and down his cheek, he closes his eyes and smiles into it. I move to his mouth, and run my thumb over his eager, pink lips.

His smile continues. He looks so open, so vulnerable, so beautiful.

I sit on his lap once more, slower and gentler than before.

Wrapping my hands around his neck, I hold us there for a moment, smiling back at his soft, flushed face.

I trace my hands down to the tie on his wrists, and release it.

"May I?" He enquires.

"I guess so." I tease, raising an eyebrow and smirking.

He wraps his arms around me too, holding me as close to his body as he can manage.

I rest one hand on the back of his neck, and the other on the small of his back, while he nuzzles my cheek.

I give him a little kiss on the temple.

"I think I need more time... this go around." Hugh mumbles.

"Take all the time you need. The world will still be there when we're done." I reassure.

Perfect Mary

"How are the exercises going, Charlie?" Mary asked me, looking over her notes like she does.

I don't say anything, and she knows why.

"So, you haven't been doing the exercises this week?" The Wise Woman enquired.

I slump in the big armchair, wishing I'd opted to lay on the floor like last session.

"Charlie... why do you think you have avoided the exercises for another week?"

Continuing to avoid her eye line, I look around her office, glancing at the many psychology textbooks, the diplomas, and the stiff but stylish furniture, finally landing on the floor.

"Would you rather lay on the floor... like our last session?" Mary finally asks.

God she's so observant and perceptive. It's annoying.

I purse my lips, and fidget, feeling her eyes on me and my body temperature rising.

"...yes."

Faster than I thought possible, I kick my shoes off, take off my jacket, and grab the cushion from the armchair.

And thank fuck, I'm staring only at the ceiling, and not the décor and status markers that make me so uncomfortable.

"Now, when you feel-"

"I feel so stupid around you." I interrupt.

"Right, and wh-"

"You're so composed and proper and you have all these fucking things all over the wall telling everyone you're so smart and insightful and fucking good at your job and it's like, I'm just this little bean, rotting in the corner."

This time Mary doesn't speak, no doubt trying to illicit more words from my spewing mouth. And fuck her, because it works every time.

"I'm so intimidated by all your smarts and you're dressed so... like an adult and I fucking come in here and I'm watched by you and it's like... yeah, that's the point, you know, I see the irony. But it's like, I wanna do some good work, for me, for you, and so I can't just go and do the exercises, because what if I do them wrong and I come back in and you look at me, like-" I turn to her with all the pain that's inside me. "... like you are right now." I sheepishly finish.

A moment breathes between us, I snap back to stare at the ceiling, but I know Mary is staring at me. I see her out the corner of my eye, and feel her curious scrutiny.

"Charlie, we have been working on your feelings around the idea of perfectionism, why do you think we haven't made much progress?"

Just like that, I'm crying. I didn't even feel it coming on, it started and suddenly my head feels full and heavy, my face feels hot, my tears feel shameful and hideous, and I feel broken and exposed to the perfect and perceptive Mary The Smarty Pants.

I turn away from her, partly so she doesn't see, and partly because I always worry crying on my back will cause some kind of brain damage. Something about the fluids not having some help from gravity makes me very anxious, and I can't afford to lose any more intelligence.

"Charlie, I urge you not to feel judged in this room. This room is for you, it's safe. It's for you to express these worries, concerns, and fears."

The all too familiar voices swell in my brain like a symphony of doubt and hurt. Telling me this isn't appropriate, this is embarrassing, I'm weak and foolish, I'm the worst of all Mary's patients, I should kill myself, and even more than that, everyone would be better off if I'd never even existed.

I just want to be in my room, in my bed, under the covers and safe.

Safe and alone, listening to The Wonder Years, mouthing the words and crying quietly. Like I used to as a teen, hoping against hope that I couldn't be heard over the music.

It's not perfect, but it's familiar. And sometimes, that feels better than opening up these wounds with Perfect Mary.

Mary places a box of tissues between me and the patients' armchair, and I hear her sit back down behind me. In her big shiny chair, no doubt.

"Charlie, please take your time, and know I'm ready when you are."

And then it clicked. I haven't cried in front of Mary before. And whenever I've cried in front of anyone else, which was a small sample size, I was never met with anything so kind and yet so **simple**.

"Mary?" I call out, still facing away from her, and staring unfocused at the bottom of the patients' armchair.

"Yes, Charlie?"

"Do you... do you care about me?"

"Of course, I care about you, Charlie. I'm here to help you. I wouldn't be very good at helping you if I didn't care."

I roll over to show Mary my teary face, but look down at my hands rather than look her in the eye.

"Do you care about all your patients?"

"Well, yes."

"Why?"

"Why in what sense, Charlie?"

"In the sense... why do you care about them? They're all broken, sad people... like me."

"Do you see yourself as broken, Charlie?"

I look up and see Mary's face is so soft. Soft in a way I've never fully taken in before. Her notes are down, she's leaning forward, open and listening. Caring.

And I suddenly don't feel as intimidated by her. Suddenly, we're just two people.

"Yes."

"Do you feel we can talk about that, Charlie?"

"Yes."

Sunshine After Rain

I place a chaste kiss on Jasmine's cheek and feel the tingles run through my body.

Pulling back, I see she's smiling, and feel myself smiling too.

We look at each for a second, and I feel a warmth radiate from my chest, running around my body, making me forget the bitter chill of the winter around us.

"Well, I'll message you." I chirp up, knowing Jasmine already said she needs to go now if she's going to make her last train.

"You better had Sarah. I'll check my phone every hour, on the hour, so if you message at five past, you'll have to wait fifty-five minutes for a reply." Jasmine stated, her expression going stony without warning.

And then, a smile.

"I'll message at two minutes to the hour then, just to be sure." I throw back.

I laugh, she laughs, it's surprisingly... fun?

Jasmine gestures that she needs to start walking, and I nod.

There's a silent acknowledgement that we both wish we could stay a little longer, stay here and keep talking, laughing, maybe have a real kiss.

But this isn't a romcom, one where we're both inexplicably wealthy enough to each pay for cabs home, after missing our last trains, and we go back to our impossibly lavish apartments, despite being average young people in a big city.

No, in our reality, we both know the extra expense of a cab fare will be felt by our grocery budget or our rent payment, so we go our separate ways, however reluctantly.

As I walk along the damp London streets, with their dark pavements, guarding my hands from the chilly air by hiding them in my pockets, I feel an unfamiliar friend returning to me.

A happiness, a hope, a joy of sorts. A friend I thought had left me, had faded from my mind, and might never return. But here they are, dancing around my brain, and lighting up all those good spots.

I reach into my tote bag, scrummaging around for my phone and headphones, both of which have managed to get lost in among old tissues, food wrappers, and two or three mini notebooks.

Managing to free them from the clutches of my clutter, I done the headphones, and plug them into my phone, unsure what music to play to mark this moment.

I wanted to feel like I was in that unrealistic romcom, even if just for the walk to Gospel Oak.

But fuck, have I been sad. Everything I'd listened to, searched for, or put into a playlist was for catharsis, for rage, for despair. Nothing for celebration, for harmony, for crushing on a hot girl.

Then it hits me: Walking On Sunshine.

I'm doing that, I'm fucking pumped, I'm absolutely walking all over that sunshine, baby! Don't even worry about it.

139

I throw on the song, and for a few seconds, the cheerful sounds don't hit my ears right. It's foreign to use music for something so positive.

It's been so long since I put on a track for celebration, rather than as a distraction, an escape, or to allow me space to express something I've been holding on to far too long.

But as the first "Ow!" kicks in, and the horns play their addictive phrase, I start to reintroduce myself to the positivity.

My shoulders move side-to-side, and I bob my head slightly as a smile spreads across my face, and the music fills my soul and warms it from the inside out.

Jasmine's face appears in my mind's eye, and my smile widens.

The start of something new, meeting someone and feeling that flutter, that spark, that sense of connection.

It's easy to forget how good it feels.

The way it electrifies the body, wakes up the brain, makes you feel unstoppable. The rush of possibility, of being able to start fresh, of knowing I can still feel this energised at all, it lights up my tired, bitter mind.

I'm excited, I'm alive, I'm still fucking here!

You can't kill me, you can't keep me down, I will meet a cute girl at the comedy night, and she will like my set, and she will think I'm worth talking to, and we'll just go and fucking hit it off!

How about that, universe!?

How about that, sadness, doubt, self-loathing? Huh? You like them apples? My rosy and flushed cheeks apple-y enough for ya?

You can't slow me down for long, I will get back up, and I will be okay.

Dear Reader,

No request to go back and read from the beginning this time.

It's a collection of flash fiction, there's not really any spoiling this time.

So, thank you for purhcasing, and reading 'Daydreamings', my first ever work of prose.

Some of these pieces feel like they were written by someone else, and others feel familiar and comforting.

What a lifetime ago 2020 feels, and yet, I was stuck there until quite recently. Time is such an odd friend, one I never quite got to know well enough, but hopefully I can get to know them soon.

I hope you enjoyed the glimpses this collection offers, and I that you saw yourself in a few of the characters, I mean there's enough to choose from, aye?

It's quite odd to only "properly" publish something more than three years after it was written, and maybe I'll regret even giving this one longer legs, but for now, I'm very flattered that you read this one, and I hope to write you another letter soon.

Kind regards,

Neptune Henriksen

Neptune Henriksen

About The Author

Neptune Henriksen is a critically acclaimed writer and theatre maker, as well as an award-winning director.

Their works explore identity, sexuality, and emotional turmoil through a queer, intersectional lens, with love, humour, and introspection.

Their art is prolific and varied, from storytelling to comedy directing, microfiction to physical theatre, with their artistic voice always shining through, unique and clear.

Their works seek to comfort, to explore, and to shed light on topics often shied away from.

Other Works By The Author

Queer Summer Trilogy, 2022-2023

Three novellas of queer romance in the Australian Summer.

1. 'Where The Pink Meets The Blue', a bisexual erotica

2. 'Under A Summer Sky In January', a sapphic teen love triangle

3. 'We Used To Hold Hands All The Time', A romance of childhood friends reunited

'Daydreamings: A Collection Of Connections', 2020

A flash fiction collection, snapshots of moments of connection and relationships of all intersections.

www.ingramcontent.com/pod-product-compliance
Lightning Source LLC
Chambersburg PA
CBHW071924130726
47909CB00014B/2572